SECRETS
IN THE
HOLLOW
A SLEEPY HOLLOW NOVEL

BARBARA DULLAGHAN

MINDSTIR MEDIA

Secrets in the Hollow
Copyright © 2023 by Barbara Dullaghan. All rights reserved.

This is a work of fiction. Names, characters, places and incidents are products of the author's imagination or are used fictitiously and should not be construed as real. Any resemblance to actual events, locales, organizations or persons, living or dead, is entirely coincidental.

No part of this book may be used or reproduced in any manner whatsoever without written permission, except in the case of brief quotations embodied in critical articles and reviews. For more information, e-mail all inquiries to info@mindstirmedia.com.

Published by Mindstir Media, LLC
45 Lafayette Rd | Suite 181| North Hampton, NH 03862 | USA
1.800.767.0531 | www.mindstirmedia.com

Front cover photo credited to JoAnn Moser

Printed in the United States of America
ISBN: XXX-X-XXXXXXX-X-X

For my parents,
Jim and Florence Brown,
and Jack

CONTENTS

PART ONE

This evening in the cemetery, the sun had just set, the moon had not yet fully risen in the sky, and a young boy's battered and bloody body lay at the feet of the Bronze Lady. Just a few minutes before he had been his usual self: a bully, obnoxious and taunting. Now, he drifted in and out of consciousness. He could hear someone whimper and call his name. He could smell the earth on which he lay and, for a brief moment when his eyes fluttered open, he could see the Bronze Lady and a glimpse of his brother before all went dark.

CHAPTER 1

AN UNEXPECTED RETURN

It stopped me in my tracks. Literally. My tracks in the crusty snow. The realization after twenty years that my mother was right and she didn't know that I had secrets.

I am always running from something.

She'd say, "You can run but you cannot hide, Carolyn."

A list of my secrets would seem ridiculously endless, as if everything in my life was frightening. But it seemed that way to me.

Once, in an uncharacteristically weak moment, Mother admitted to me how sad she felt that I hadn't married and borne children, as if I couldn't have them without being married. Almost gave myself away then.

I am always running from something.

My feet were getting cold so I headed back to my house. Although it was early March, Plattsburgh's location ten miles from the Canadian border still meant deep snow on the ground.

Would I ever tell my mother that she had been right? For God's sake. At forty years old, am I still worried about not telling her everything? I rounded the corner by my house and those thoughts about my mother were suddenly interrupted.

I noticed a police car and two officers standing outside my front door.

Is it happening? Now? I stopped abruptly and then slowly walked toward them. "Can I help you, officers?"

The burly cop with a dark black mustache turned to face me. "We are looking for Carolyn Peters. Is that you?"

"Yes, what's wrong? What happened?"

"I am Officer Cardell and this is Officer Simon. We're with the Plattsburgh Police Department," he said, as they flashed their badges. "May we talk with you inside?"

"Why?" I said as I fumbled with the keys to unlock the door.

"Are you the daughter of Philip and Marjorie Peters of Sleepy Hollow, New York?"

"Yes, please tell me what is going on."

The next twenty minutes were a blur of alarming images of a deadly crash with another car, presumably someone running a stop sign and plowing head on into my parents. As if to comfort me, the officer assured me they died instantly.

This is unbelievable. Such a shock but it could have been worse. Right? Oh, God, how can I think that way? My parents are dead. Terrible way to die.

My hands started to shake uncontrollably; then I burst into tears. The burly cop asked, "Miss Peters, are you OK? Can we get you anything? John," he said to the other cop, "get her a glass of water." After placing the water on the table, he also put a throw blanket over my knees.

They waited until my neighbor came to keep me company and left me sitting in my favorite chair. She stayed with me, respecting my silence.

"I never got to say goodbye," I said to her. "I never got to resolve our issues."

"I'm sure they knew how much you loved them," she said.
Did they?

My mother had it right. I would always be running from something.

Before I left Plattsburgh for the funeral, my principal found a substitute teacher for my fifth-grade class. I locked up my two-bedroom house and left. No plants to water, no pets to feed or walk. I am enough. Thank God for Zoloft.

I drove the five hours to my hometown, Sleepy Hollow, a little village twenty miles north of New York City on the Hudson River. I pulled into the driveway of my parents' home, a two-story brick colonial with large columns, larger than most in the Philips Manor neighborhood. I felt my chest tighten every time I came home as an adult. I always thought that my parents tried to make a statement of their wealth.

The first time I walked through their house when I returned to town, I actually held onto the walls to keep me upright. All the memories of a scared girl starting a new life seemed to come back at once. My first day at a new school as a senior in high school, hoping no one would know there had been a scandal with my father and his secretary.

Within an hour of my arriving home Nessa, my best friend since high school, showed up to give me one of her very aggressive, all-encompassing hugs.

Before she could even speak, I said, "I'm not sure how long I'll stay, Nessa. Don't get your hopes up."

Nessa's eyebrows furrowed as she backed away to look at me and then came in for another hug.

"Yeah, yeah. I'm just glad you're here, Mija."

Hearing her call me *Mija* made me feel even more at home. It's a term of endearment to Puerto Ricans and Nessa had called me that since high school.

It had been a long time since I lived in town so Nessa, notorious for never taking time off from her job as a police officer, used three days of personal time to help me navigate writing my parents' obituary for the town newspaper, making the funeral and burial arrangements, planning the luncheon after, and even helping me choose the music to be played. The first thing on our list involved walking across Route 9 from my parents' home to Sleepy Hollow Cemetery to discuss the arrangements. As we entered the driveway and approached the big iron gates, I slowed down and broke into a sweat. Nessa turned around.

"Mija, what's the matter? The office is right up here."

"Yeah, I know. I just need a minute to gather my thoughts."

"You look terrible," Nessa said. "I can't imagine this whole thing is easy. Believe me, I'm not looking forward to it at all when my parents pass."

I nodded. But Nessa didn't know the whole story.

We trudged through the open gates that were bordered by two walkways under stone archways, also gated. Straight ahead were the ivy-covered offices, built with gray and yellow stone. The colors struck me as beautiful but didn't ease my mind.

During the meeting, I felt distracted thinking about my parents being buried together. There had been a scandal and I could feel a bit of empathy for my mother.

Hmm. Maybe Mother and Father will not be together like I imagined.

"Carrie?" I felt Nessa's hand on my arm, bringing me back to the conversation. "They need a check for the fees."

"Oh, sorry. Sure."

After we finished with our paperwork, Nessa said, "Let's visit your Aunt Susan's grave. That might help a little to see the place where your parents will be buried before the funeral."

We walked over to the gravesite. My parents would be buried in the Donahue family plot, defined by metal bars outlining the perimeter of the rectangular property. As I looked down on my aunt's grave, I smiled hoping the sisters were reunited. My mother had desperately missed her sister after she died so unexpectedly from breast cancer at forty-seven years old.

Nessa wanted to walk through the grounds. We admired the huge old oak and maple trees, which were just budding and not giving even a hint of their dazzling orange and yellow colors that would come in the fall.

"I don't get the chance to walk through here very often," Nessa said. "Did you ever hear about some of the historical figures buried here?"

"Well, of course I know about Washington Irving and the Old Dutch Church," I said. "But not too much more."

"Andrew Carnegie, one of the world's wealthiest people, is buried up here on the right. The Astors' graves are behind the mausoleum. I wonder if you know whose grave this is."

I stopped to look at the grave with the name Elizabeth N. Graham. "How funny," I said. "It only has the date of her death, not her birth."

"Have you heard of Elizabeth Arden? This is her grave. She never told people her age. I guess that's the beauty business."

Not paying attention to our path, suddenly we stood in a place I remembered. I blinked in surprise. There stood the Bronze Lady, an imposing statue marking a gravesite. A distant memory in my hazy mind.

"Oh my God. I feel like I'm going to pass out. Nessa, I..." I said, as I reached toward her.

"Carrie, you're so pale! Here, lean against this rock 'til you catch your breath."

After a few minutes of quiet, waiting for the dizziness to stop, Nessa said, "Feel better? This is too much for you. Let's get home so you can rest."

On the way back to the house, I heard someone call my name from behind.

"Carrie! Is that you?"

I turned around but it took a moment before I recognized him. Still tall and gangly, Chester VanWert had graduated with us. I remembered how he went to the cemetery almost every day in high school, always alone.

"Hi, Nessa," Chester said. "Carrie, so sorry to hear about your parents. Are you home to stay?"

How weird is that? His voice still sounds the same, a high pitch.

Nessa jumped into the conversation.

"Carrie's feeling a bit under the weather, Chester. How about if we talk another time?"

"Oh, sure. I'll call you, Nessa. How about next week?"

"Goodbye, Chester," Nessa said.

"OK. Don't forget. Bye." Chester stumbled as he backed up.

When we got back to my house, Nessa helped me into my car. "I have coffee at my place." We began the short drive to Nessa's house in Tarrytown.

I hadn't really taken the time to look around when I first returned to the villages. My only goal had been to get to my parents' house. Now, sitting in the passenger seat, I looked at the towns for the first time through mindful eyes. The villages were composed of Tarrytown to the south and Sleepy Hollow, formerly known as North Tarrytown, to the North.

On the right as we left Philips Manor, we passed the historic site of Philipsburg Manor, a historic museum commemorating a gristmill and trading complex built in 1750.

Driving down tree-lined Route 9 south, I glanced at Sleepy Hollow High School up on the hill to the left. The home of the Headless Horsemen, our school mascot. How many other secrets did that school hold besides mine?

Entering Tarrytown, Patriot's Park came up next on the right with the statue of Major John Andre and the lovely big tulip trees and shallow, slow-moving creek.

"I remember seeing Bobby Kennedy there in the park when he was running for the New York Senate," I told Nessa.

"I was there too!" she said. "But that was before you moved here, right?"

"Yeah. My parents were so excited, especially when Bobby shook my hand. I felt giddy, as if I were meeting a rock star. Pretty amazing moment in my life."

Nessa nodded. "That was pretty cool for our little town."

Right after the park came Warner Library built in 1929. Nessa and I spent many hours in the library, supposedly doing homework but spending most of our time flirting with boys.

We entered the business district in Tarrytown and I was struck by the narrowness of Route 9, especially with cars parked on each side of the street. As a high schooler though, those narrow streets had helped me feel safe, at least for a while. I let out a deep sigh.

"Almost there," said Nessa. She parked in the driveway of her two-toned green, two-bedroom home.

As the coffee brewed, I felt my body start to relax and feel the warmth of the sun in her kitchen. I had a flashback to sitting in Nessa's mother's kitchen where the family drank strong coffee with a tiny bit of sugar and milk, *café con leche*. The coffee always smelled inviting, with aromas of chocolate and caramel. I didn't drink coffee at home; it was never offered. But I enjoyed it on Saturday mornings at Nessa's.

"I can see you relaxing, Mija. Your body seems to be melting into the chair."

"Yeah, this coffee is amazing," I said. "Do you know where we could find a bagpiper? My father always loved them."

"I actually think I do. Danny's father belongs to the Knights of Columbus who hired one last year for an event. I'll ask him."

My heart skipped a beat hearing Danny's name. I looked away from Nessa and whispered his name.

"Danny."

At the service two days later, about thirty of my parents' new and old friends and colleagues came to honor them at Transfiguration Church in Tarrytown. There were many bouquets of colorful flowers on and around the altar and the priest delivered a brief but flattering eulogy. My parents had donated often to the church.

The bagpiper played at the cemetery. The sounds were haunting and I hoped my parents could hear the music in heaven. I couldn't help but remember how my father loved to sing the song and its lyric to the Irish classic, "Danny Boy."

Suddenly I felt conflicted about honoring my father. The music sounded grating. *Wish the bagpiper would finish. I hate this song.*

As the funeral came to an end, I placed two red roses, my mother's favorite, on their coffins before they were lowered. As I leaned on Nessa with our heads together, I whispered that I had become an orphan, with no one in the world to love me.

Nessa gasped and I turned to look in the direction where she looked. There stood the person I once loved, although I hadn't seen him in twenty years. Danny. He returned my gaze with a sad smile, and turned to leave the gravesite.

CHAPTER 2

FRESH START

When I moved to Sleepy Hollow to start my senior year of high school, I made a huge decision. No more being called Carolyn, no more filling my life with just studies and the flute, and no more being friends with only those people my parents felt were appropriate. I plastered "Fresh Start" in big yellow letters across the huge bulletin board in my bedroom.

My parents had promised things would be different with this move. My father would be "more present" and my mother "more attentive." If only they realized that wasn't all I needed. I needed a release from the anxiety of trying to be the perfect child.

When I was six years old, the family made our first move from Morningside Heights in Manhattan to Scarsdale, New York. My father had finished his master's degree in history at Columbia and had taken a job with IBM, an up-and-coming computer firm, in an upscale NYC suburb. He had risen quickly up the ranks due to his easy smile and cigar-smoking friends at his exclusive country club.

But Mother was much more complicated. Before I was born, she said she filled her days in Morningside Heights keeping their small apartment warm, clean, and cheery and preparing dinners while waiting for my father to return home. She enjoyed their coffee time in the mornings before he left her alone for the day.

She told me later on that she always felt challenged to keep herself busy, buying the paper every day and scouring the society pages, making mental notes to remember certain items when Father graduated, and struggling with the realization that it felt important to her. Father probably just listened to her babble when he came home, but Mother told me his attention to his newspaper took priority.

When I was born on that glorious morning in July, it seemed the world had finally given my mother a worthy purpose. She had suffered three miscarriages and the realization that she had carried me to term had been overwhelming to her and Father.

Mother and I were cleaning my room one Saturday when she recounted one of their first conversations as parents when the nurse placed me on the bed next to my tiny clothes and left the room.

"We just couldn't believe you were really there," Mother told me. "Your father finally told me he thought we should dress you but I thought we should just wait until the nurse came back."

And so they waited and marveled at my rosy cheeks and big blue eyes. And waited, until the nurse returned about twenty minutes later.

"Don't you want to go home?" the nurse asked. "That baby can't dress herself! Now, get on with it. She's not gonna break," the nurse chuckled as she left the room, chubby hands on wide hips mumbling something that sounded like, "Oh, boy."

"And she was right," Mother said. "You wouldn't break if I took good care with your skinny arms and legs."

But my mother told me in confidence that day, "I was always petrified I would do something to hurt you." She never admitted that to Father though who said she took to it naturally.

Their fascination with Tarrytown began with visits to Sleepy Hollow Cemetery to leave flowers on the grave of my mother's Aunt Susan. I always liked going to the cemetery. I know a lot of people feel uncomfortable there but I've always been fascinated with the whole ritual of remembering the dead. Anyway, moving to Sleepy Hollow didn't surprise me and change seemed like a good thing at the time.

Nessa Martinez became my first and best friend at Sleepy Hollow High. We had gym class together and, that first day in September, the teacher told us that we needed to find locker partners. Nessa turned to me, pointed, and said, "You." I just nodded, a little intimidated and, from then on, we were always together. She had plenty of other friends but she said she was just drawn to me. She thought I needed a friend.

Nessa had been born and raised in Tarrytown, after her grandparents emigrated from Puerto Rico. I admired her curly black hair, huge brown eyes and olive skin. She was almost the same height as me but with an athletic body. There weren't many opportunities to play girls' sports but she played on the basketball team. Nessa was also an only child, but extended family filled Nessa's life. I visited her house on Wildey Street many times. The family rolled up the carpet in the living room and everyone danced. That would never have happened in my house and I don't know how my parents would have reacted to it. It probably would have made them very uncomfortable. I remember just clapping to the music and watching everyone's faces until Nessa dragged me up to dance.

Nessa's family attended St. Teresa's Catholic Church every Sunday morning for mass and then came home to a meal prepared by her Mama and Abuela. It was a feast for the senses: mouth-watering plates of colorful food, enticing smells, lots of hugging and people laughing over loud music.

Nessa's family had an old bulldog named Old Blue Eyes after Frank Sinatra. They called him Blue. Slow moving and fat, he always made me smile even when he slobbered on me.

Nessa and I slept over at each other's houses at least once every weekend. We set each other's long hair with orange juice cans and then tried to sleep on them. Nessa's hair was super curly and mine, wavy. When the cans didn't work, we ironed each other's hair, placing a thin towel between the hair and an iron.

Occasionally, Nessa had a sleepover with five or six other girls. I found it fascinating to listen to all these girls gossip and share secrets. Almost an outsider, I didn't have their shared history and didn't understand all the stories. A few would say a few phrases in Spanish and I would nudge Nessa for help.

"Ah, that Billy is a *mamalon*!" They all giggled.

Nessa whispered to me, "He's a mama's boy." I laughed and agreed.

The girls always asked me about Danny, a boy I dated. Were they happy for me or just trying to get some gossip? Nessa got them to change the subject away from me when she saw me wiping my hands on my pajamas. I went into the bathroom before I started shaking. I did not like being the center of attention and Nessa knew it.

Nessa and I liked to talk about the future. It had always been expected by my parents that I would go to a four-year college, probably to become a teacher. I was fine with that idea. I thought it would be great to live away from my parents but almost constantly worried about all that came with it: dorm life, having a roommate, not having Nessa or Danny nearby. There were lots of things to worry about and Nessa tried to ease my mind.

"We'll talk every week and you can come home to visit once a month," she promised.

I agreed and nodded my head emphatically. "Of course, we will. And then, I'll come back after college to teach."

Nessa's plans centered around attending Westchester Community College to study police science and then the police academy in New Rochelle, hoping to serve in the Tarrytown Police Department along with her father. I didn't think there was any question that Nessa would live and work anywhere else. Or that she would make a great police officer. She exuded confidence and, when she walked, led with her chin. I did not like that she smoked cigarettes. But I'm sure she hated that I bit my nails down to the quick. I hoped those habits would change with age.

I fell for Danny right away when we met in high school. My new friends were telling me that we were the "it couple." Nessa said that girls were jealous of me.

"How lucky you are," they said.

Danny seemed different to me from the beginning. I knew he played football but he didn't act conceited or attention-grabbing. I noticed Danny in a few of my classes because of his dimples but we didn't talk until that day in the hall when he saw me standing with two of his friends.

"Hey, Danny," one of them said. "Did you meet the new girl?"

The guys laughed behind their hands as Danny stammered a croaking hello. So sweet. I couldn't help it. I reached out to touch his arm and tried to smile. He actually blushed.

Danny called me every day after football practice. He first asked me out to go for pizza after a football game.

Nessa and I went to the first football game of the season together. I parked my car and we started walking across the grass on the left side of the school, Washington Irving Junior High.

"I don't see the field, Nessa," I said. "I can sure hear the crowd though."

The crowd was yelling, "Hoorah for Horsemen, hoo-rah for Horsemen, someone in the crowd is yelling hoorah for Horsemen..."

"Just wait," she answered.

We walked across the lawn and could see the glistening blue water of the Hudson River. As we got to the edge of the lawn, I gasped. Right below us, granite seating had been built into the hill down to the playing field. The teams were doing drills on the field. It was very impressive for a high school game.

Nessa and I joined a bunch of classmates and I looked around. I'll bet there were a thousand people seated in the stands and standing at the top. I quickly joined in and cheered on Danny, Jake, and the rest of the Horsemen with the cheerleaders. It was a close game but we won. I knew Danny would be in a great mood.

After the game, Nessa and I walked to Johnny's Pizza on Main Street to save a table for Danny and Jake, Nessa's boyfriend and Danny's best friend. I looked around at my new friends and felt really happy that we had moved to Sleepy Hollow. Danny even held my hand under the table.

After just a few dates, Danny admitted something to me.

"I remember the first time I saw you, Carrie. My ma always told me I have a gift for the words, but I had no words, nothing. Speechless. When you put your hand on my arm, I felt electricity!"

I couldn't help but laugh at that but he insisted. My stomach turned flips, so nervous and excited that I found this great guy.

Danny and I also shared band class together. I liked that he played sports but loved that he played the saxophone. When he brought me home to meet his parents, they had '50s music playing really loud in his house and everyone always seemed to enjoy being together, talking and laughing over each other. Walking me back to my car that night, we stopped under a large weeping willow tree and shared our first kiss.

Danny was my first boyfriend and I was not used to spending time with a group of boys. I did notice that his friends were kind of jerks to kids who weren't in their group. Although Danny didn't join in, he didn't tell them to stop, and seemed kind of embarrassed about it when I was around. Jake also tried to avoid it but Jake's little brother Timmy was obnoxious. He reminded me of a peacock I had seen in a zoo when I was little and never forgot. Always trying to get noticed. Always the loudest. Always the meanest.

Danny's parents owned Clooney's Tavern in Tarrytown and he worked weekends there, washing and putting away dishes. While his friends and I loved spending time there, it became stifling to Danny, who was starting to sense and hope his destiny did not include the restaurant.

"I've spent almost every day of my life in there and, at seventeen, that's enough. Ma wants me to go away to college, but only if I come home again. How can I promise that? I know my brother Kevin's here but he told me he's leaving as soon as he can."

Danny looked at me. "I'm so glad I met you. I needed to get my heart racing again." When I smiled, he pulled me toward him, and I was surprised that it seemed a little rough to me.

Danny had been raised spending Sunday mornings at St. Teresa's Church and the afternoons with his family at his grandmother's small house on Depeyster Street. Many of Grandma's eighteen children and their families showed up at different times of the day to eat and talk loudly to be heard over the chaos in her home.

"My grandparents' family received an award for 'the largest family in Westchester County' and my father said they all got new shoes as a gift," Danny said. "So exciting for them."

Danny, one of the oldest grandchildren, adored his grandmother and loved spending time with her. He still missed his grandfather, who died when Danny was four.

"He taught me how to play checkers," Danny said with a grin.

"I really had no relationship with my grandparents," I said. "They all died young."

"Sorry about that, Carrie."

I snuggled a little closer to him. "Tell me more, Danny."

"The cousins played outside," Danny said. "Inside, my aunts were busy with babies and the kitchen and the men watched television, arguing and yelling at the kids to quiet down. Everyone drank highballs."

I found it very hard to imagine that life. My home had three people, three very quiet people. Three very introverted people who barely talked because we feared any confrontation or disagreement. My heart started to pound remembering sitting down to dinner with them. Of course, most of the attention was on me. It had to be different in a larger family, I hoped.

Danny continued. "Outside on Depeyster Street, my younger cousins played kickball and all the little girls giggled on the steps about who they were going to marry. My Aunt Florence and Aunt Gail always came out on the porch to lead the girls in a sing-a-long. I even joined them a few times."

"What songs did you like to sing?" I asked.

"I sang Buddy Holly and some Elvis when I was little," Danny said. He looked at me and we both laughed at the thought. "But I knew my time had come when the little ones started a girl band called Cookie and the Crumbles. I got outta there!"

Getting his heart racing always seemed to be something that Danny needed. He and his friends had been involved in some silly dares back in middle and high school. Danny said they started out by trying to find the Bronze Lady, one of the spooky tales of Sleepy Hollow Cemetery, right up there with the Headless Horseman and Ichabod Crane.

Danny said later that his whole life changed because of the Bronze Lady. I listened wide-eyed as Danny told me the story.

"Have you ever heard of the Bronze Lady, Carrie?" I shook my head.

"I can't believe you've never heard of her. The Bronze Lady is legendary here. She's over a hundred years old and sits in a creepy little courtyard with an old crypt for a Civil War general. Spooky as hell. But my cousin warned me not to spit on her."

"Why not? It's just a statue," I said.

"Too much has happened to people who disrespected her. Another cousin of mine said he spit on her and got into a car crash the next day and broke his arm. Couldn't play ball for the rest of the season."

"That's scary. What else do people say?"

"One story says she comes to life at night and wanders the cemetery. Another says if you knock on the door of the General's crypt, you'll have bad dreams that night. The worst, I think, is if you dare sit on the lady's lap, she will cry tears of blood!"

"Ooh, so creepy," I said, my shoulders shaking.

"My life seemed so boring," Danny admitted to me. "So I decided to check it out with my seventh grade buddy, Rick, and my brother Kevin. I told them we were just going to find The Bronze Lady, look at her, and run back to the stone wall. That's what we agreed."

"But things did not go totally as we planned," Danny continued. "After our parents and youngest brother went to bed, Kevin and I snuck out of our house and met up with Rick outside Douglas Park. My cousin had given me some Boone's Farm for us to celebrate. You know, that cheap wine? Anyway, after climbing over the stone wall in the park, Rick and I took off through the brush, down the steep hill, and over the wooden footbridge that crossed the stream, and left Kevin to deal with the flinging branches.

"We heard Kevin yell and then it got quiet. Kevin had tripped over a downed branch and fell face-first into the damp yuck. Of course, we had to go back to get him. He was spitting out pieces of dirt and sticks. Pretty funny."

I felt like I could taste the dirt and sticks. I knew that Danny was telling the truth when he talked about the quiet of the cemetery at night. I could visualize the heavy overgrown trees on each side of the stream and how they hid the partial moon and clear skies. I also believed him when he told me that no one wanted to admit that he was scared.

"It took us about ten minutes to walk to the Rockefeller Mausoleum, close to the Lady," Danny continued. "None of us were talking. It was spooky quiet until Rick pointed to her.

"You've never seen her. Right?"

"Right," I said.

"Well, I'm sure my mouth was hangin' open. She is something else! The Bronze Lady is huge with these great big arms and hands. It's creepy 'cause she's sitting between these two trees, just facing a crypt. None of us could move. But then, without saying a word, damn Rick changed the plan and touched her. So, Kevin and I touched her and ran for our lives and did not wait to see what happened. We just wanted out of that cemetery."

Danny said he didn't look back when he dropped the paper bag with the wine. They ran down the steep hills, sliding on damp grass and grabbing onto branches to slow themselves down a bit until they finally retraced their steps over the wooden bridge, back up the muddy hill, and reached the wall into Douglas Park.

"We all screamed in unison as we crossed back over the stone wall, breathin' hard and bursting with macho," Danny continued. "We made a pact to return every month and push our dare a bit further. But, as things happened, Rick and his family moved the following month and, you know, I just got too busy."

Was that really the reason?

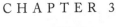

CHAPTER 3

REVELATIONS

A few days after the funeral on a gloomy and overcast day, Nessa suggested we dine at Clooney's Tavern on Main in Tarrytown. Nessa found a parking spot and we crossed the street. Turning my head to the left, I glimpsed the shimmering blue of the Hudson River, an ever-present reminder that I had left Plattsburgh.

Walking through the heavy wooden door of Clooney's made me think I entered a time machine. My eyes slowly adjusted to the darkness of the room. Above the bar hung the dusty painted sign that had been there since the bar opened in 1948, *Cead Mile Failte*, "A Hundred Thousand Welcomes." I noticed the glistening bar made of wood veneer with mahogany stain, small green and yellow bags of Wise potato chips hanging on a stand, and the liquor bottles lined up under a large mirror on the wall. Just like twenty years ago.

"Oh, now there's a face I've missed seeing!" the owner, Mr. Clooney said. "*Failte*! It pained me to hear about your parents. So sad, so young." I couldn't hide my smile as the now gray-haired, barrel chested man came around the bar to give me one of his wrap-around hugs.

"You have been missed, young lady," he said. "And *Beannu* to you, Nessa."

"Thank you so much. I had to come in for your famous corned beef on rye with all the fixings," I said, quickly changing the subject.

"Coming right up! Nessa, your usual?"

"Yes, sir!"

We slid into a booth and just listened to the sound coming from the best jukebox in the county for oldies. I closed my eyes and my body swayed to "The Sounds of Silence" until Mr. Clooney's voice and chuckle jolted me back to reality.

"And, what would you ladies like to drink? Cherry Coke, Carrie?"

"Absolutely. Bring all the memories back at once."

"You know," I said to Nessa. "It's so dark in here and those old black and white pictures are still on the walls. It's all actually a bit comforting."

Nessa pointed to a few of the pictures of townspeople and then stopped at one, looking down at the table.

"Nessa, is something the matter?" I asked.

She looked up at me with a grim smile. "This one," she pointed. "This one is kind of special."

I inched up to examine it more closely. Four young teenage boys posed in front of The Music Hall, the oldest theater in Westchester County. They stood in front of and partially blocked a movie poster and held what looked like glasses in their hands.

At the top of the poster it read, "13 times the thrills! 13 times the screams! 13 times the fun!"

"What movie was that?" I asked. "The title is blocked."

Nessa laughed. "You can't tell from the byline…13, 13, 13? It's *13 Ghosts*!"

"I remember hearing about that movie," I said. "Of course, my parents didn't allow me to go. Why does this picture upset you?"

"Well, the boys are Jake, Timmy, Danny, and Kevin."

"Oh, that's sad." I backed away from the picture.

"It is," Nessa said. "Hard to believe two of them are gone."

"Mmm hmm."

We went back to our plates of food. I felt like I devoured my sandwich and fries in two bites and excused myself to go to the restroom.

The restroom also hadn't changed much in twenty years. The last time I was there, I saw degrading curse words next to the names of girls. There were also initials of couples scraped into hearts. But the panels in the stalls had been replaced and they remained clean, for now.

As I returned to the booth, I noticed the back of the head of another person sitting in my seat and Nessa trying to catch my attention, her dark brown eyes growing larger by the second.

Hmm. Who's that?

As I turned to slide into the booth next to Nessa, the music seemed to slow down and the light seemed to dim as I looked into Danny's upturned face. His eyes brightened and as he started to speak.

"Hi, Carrie. Been a long time."

"Oh, no," I said and walked out of the bar and kept on going, finally stopping to hold on to the nearest lamppost. Nessa found me bent in half, shaking, struggling to breathe in the midst of a full-blown panic attack.

She pulled me into a hug. "Carrie, what the hell? It's been over twenty years. I know it hurt when he left you in Plattsburgh but you should have seen his mouth drop when you ran out."

But I couldn't speak. He still looked damn good. He still took my breath away.

"If it makes you feel better, he never married either," Nessa said.

But Nessa didn't know everything. I turned away from her and started walking.

"I'm going home," I said over my shoulder.

I heard the sky rumble and started to count, "*One, one thousand. Two, two thousand, three…*" I turned around to see the lightning bolt flash across the sky to the south.

Good. I'm going north.

I started to do what I did best, this time in the pouring rain. I ran. I began to howl and my sobbing wracked my body, the tears mixing with the hard driving rain.

Reaching the inside of my house, I stripped down and dressed in warm sweats and heavy socks. After that, I took a sleeping pill to knock me out and calm my still shaking hands.

Because I was an only child, I thought the reading of the will would be quick and easy. I always wished I had siblings. I think I would have liked the camaraderie. I sat in my car until the last moment before my appointment, then shuffled to the door of the law office, "F. Morgan, Attorney at Law." I found Mr. Morgan's office downstairs in his imposing home in the Crest, high up on the hill in Tarrytown. The room was decorated in the colors of Notre Dame, his alma mater. He came back to New York and received his law degree at Fordham. Mr. Morgan had been my father's best friend and I had heard countless stories about their times together. He had always been Uncle Frank to me. His secretary said he would be out in a few minutes.

Another woman sat in the waiting room reading a magazine. She appeared about ten years younger than I and was dressed in a classic black dress, accented with pearl earrings and a necklace. Her makeup looked impeccable. But when she glanced up to look at me and I smiled my closed-mouth smile, she just looked away and went back to the magazine in her lap.

What's her deal? I sat down to wait.

As Uncle Frank opened the door, I noticed his face redden as I approached.

"Oh, Uncle Frank," I said.

"Carolyn. Lovely to see you again."

His hug enveloped me. It felt like hugging my father again.

I quickly glanced around the office, which had dark wood paneling with light green painting on the walls. Large windows behind Uncle Frank's desk revealed a beautiful view of the Hudson River. I also noticed a small bar set up in the corner of the office.

"Well, come on in," he said, walking to his desk. "You look well."

"Thank you, Uncle Frank. I didn't get to tell you at the funeral how much my father appreciated your friendship over the years."

"Yes, well...Phil was a good friend to me too. You know, you go through a lot when you know someone your whole life. He helped me through a lot of scrapes when we were younger."

He chuckled and wiped a tear from his eye. "I remember the time we were playing baseball and the ball went through old Mr. Pete's window. I hit the ball but he took the blame because he knew my dad would let me have it." He smiled and shook his head.

He quickly opened the first folder on his desk.

"Carolyn, I need to share something with you before we start. It is the main reason that I called you in. How much did you know about your father's life?"

At this point, the fingers on my left hand began to pick at the ones on my right. *How much would anyone know about their father's life? I know a little about his childhood, his work, and his hobbies. I know about his relationship with my mother and the scandal.*

"The reason I bring this up is because if you were the only beneficiary, I would normally just do this over the phone, but ..."

"What do you mean?" I asked. "There's another beneficiary?"

"I am sorry that your father did not share this with you, Carolyn. But Phil had another child who he had been supporting."

"What?" My upper body straightened away from him.

"I can imagine that this is a shock. I really thought your father would have told you. As close as we were as friends, Phil did not confide in me until very recently when we met to change the will. So, this surprised me."

I looked out the window over his shoulder. *No, my father never told me! No, my perfect parents never told me!*

"Did my mother know?"

"Your father told me that she did not know. He came in about six months ago to add an addendum to the will. He kept some of his money from his bonuses over the years to support the child. Obviously, he had another bank account, which he included in the addendum. But I have no idea if she suspected. He covered his tracks pretty well. I imagine he felt they had more time," Uncle Frank said.

Hmm. I guess the whole family had secrets. I knew about the mistress and the scandal, but didn't know about a child.

"So, your sister is in the lobby waiting to join us. Are you ready?"

"That woman in the waiting room is my sister?"

Uncle Frank nodded. "Her name is Stephanie Conway, twenty-six years old. She lives with her mother and step-father in Briarcliff." Briarcliff was just ten minutes north of Sleepy Hollow. It shocked me to find out that she lived so close, although I guess the proximity made it easier for my father to drop in.

"I'd like to bring her in. Are you ready?"

"I don't know if I can do this right now. I really don't." I quickly turned around to look at the door and my eyes landed on the bar.

Uncle Frank pushed away from his desk and walked around to me.

"How can I help you?" he asked.

"I think I need a drink. Do you have any whiskey over there?"

"Sure, Carolyn. I don't blame you. But are you sure?"

The clock read two o'clock in the afternoon, not a good time to start drinking.

I listened as the ice clinked in the glass and Uncle Frank poured the whiskey.

Do I really need a drink?

"Wait, Uncle Frank. How about ice water instead?"

He handed me a large glass of water and I took a long drink. "OK, I'm ready now."

Stephanie came through the door, sat in the chair next to mine, and never looked in my direction.

"Glad to meet you, Miss Conway," Uncle Frank said. "This is—"

"I know who she is," she interrupted.

"Nice to meet you," I said, extending my right hand.

Stephanie turned away. *OK, so much for being the bigger person.*

"Well," Uncle Frank said. "May I call you Stephanie?"

She nodded.

"I assume you know that you are here because you have been named as a beneficiary in Philip and Marjorie Peters' will."

"When he died, my mother admitted to me that he was my father," Stephanie said. "What a sleaze. My mother cried but I'm not too pleased about it. Seems like everyone lied to me."

"If it's any consolation, I just found out about you five minutes ago," I said. "Lying to me too."

"Humph."

I looked at Uncle Frank with my mouth hanging open and eyebrows furrowed. *What is her problem?*

"Ladies, let's get on with the reading of the will. Carolyn, you will receive the bulk of the estate which includes the house and its contents. The bonds, savings, and mutual funds also go to you. As of today, that amounts to just shy of five million dollars. Of course, you understand the markets change constantly but the value of the house and property should stay stable. Stephanie, you will keep the boat and—"

"Boat? My father had a boat?" I felt like I screamed.

So much I didn't know about my father. *How much time did he waste away from my mother on that boat?*

"Tell her that our father gave my mother and me a boat that is docked at the Westerly Marina in Ossining," Stephanie said.

Oh, my God. Will this never end? "Please, Uncle Frank. Go on."

"To continue, Stephanie will receive the boat and the money set aside for the maintenance and upkeep. The funds in the account plus the value of the boat as of today total over $400,000. Of course, if you choose, you may use the money as you see fit."

Stephanie bristled a bit in her seat and her back stiffened.

"Carolyn, I will give you the paperwork if you would like to retain another lawyer."

"No, Uncle Frank. I need you to remain my lawyer but I would like to set up a time to go over all of the estate."

"Of course," he said, with a sad smile. "We can go over specifics then. Stephanie, do you have any questions?"

"No, but I think the division of the assets is entirely unacceptable. You will be hearing from my lawyer."

And, with that, she stood up and walked out of the office, her nose in the air.

After two weeks, my school called to ask when I would be returning to my teaching job. I made the decision to return to Plattsburgh. I would keep my parents' home for the time being. At this point, I was filled with dread that it would always feel like their home. Telling Nessa would not be easy so I just spoke fast before she could argue.

"This is for the best. Of course, I'll keep the house and come down on breaks. And I'll be here for the summer. I just miss the kids in my class and I want to finish the school year with them."

"I'm glad you're keeping the house," Nessa said, looking away.

I felt relaxed driving back to Plattsburgh, although I did feel a pang of regret as I crossed the Tappan Zee Bridge. Looking to my right to glance at the villages, a thought flashed through my mind that maybe I wouldn't come back. Running away was what I did best.

Back in Plattsburgh, I settled into my "life-before-everything -changed," as I called it. I varied my daily run to right after the sun set for the day. I ran through the college campus, passed the dorms and turned onto a side street that led to the fraternity and sorority houses. When I heard a car coming behind me, I started to wave it by with my left hand but it wouldn't pass me. Fear of getting hit on the narrow street caused me to turn around to my left to wave again. The windows were dark on the deep blue sedan so I couldn't see the driver. I could not understand why it hung behind me; my mind flooded with what-ifs and what I should do if anything happened. My heart started to flutter even faster and, in a split-second decision, I turned around and ran straight past the car. As I turned and looked back, the car continued to drive down the road.

Am I imagining things? Calm down.

I finished my run and vowed not to run down that street again.

Unfortunately, six weeks later, I received a letter that my teaching position had been terminated for the following year and I discovered that no other districts were hiring. I resigned myself to return to Sleepy Hollow, at least for a while. Maybe I would look for a job elsewhere. Start a life somewhere else. Fresh start.

But talking to Nessa encouraged me to think it might be fun to live back in Sleepy Hollow. Or at least tolerable.

"It's great you'll be back here!" said Nessa over the phone. "How soon?"

"Don't rush me. The Plattsburgh house has to go on the market and I need to pack. Maybe for July 4?"

"Well, you know I'll be here for you," Nessa said. "I hope you'll be here for the fourth. The villages have a big parade. Lots of fun. I've missed you. See you soon."

I wish I felt as positive as Nessa did. I would have to find some new running routes.

Before I left Plattsburgh, I wanted to saying goodbye to my therapist of fifteen years, Anna Baker. I hadn't spoken to her since before my parents' death.

"How are you feeling about their deaths, Carrie?" she asked.

"I have to tell you that I'm not sure how I feel. At the will reading, I discovered that I have a half-sister. I thought that we left that all behind us when we moved to Sleepy Hollow."

"What was all behind you?"

"Guess I never told you the reason we moved to Sleepy Hollow in the first place. My father had an affair with his secretary. He kept his job but we moved out of the community because of the gossip."

"I see. How did it feel meeting your sister?" Anna said.

"Oh, very weird. She wouldn't look at me and is probably going to dispute the will. Don't think we'll be close," I said, laughing.

"I'm sorry about that, Carrie. How do you feel about moving back to your family home?"

"There is a lot to do but my friend Nessa has assured me it will be wonderful!"

We both smiled.

"May I speak honestly, Carrie?"

I nodded slowly.

"I have always felt that we have only been treating your symptoms of anxiety. Your relationship with anxiety has improved because of your running and the medication, but I don't know that you will ever feel totally well until you share everything with someone."

"What do you mean?" *How did she see through me?*

"I have always felt you were holding back," Anna said. "In therapy, that is your prerogative, Carrie. But I hope that you find someone to whom you can open up after your move."

Don't think I will.

"I have enjoyed getting to know you, Carrie," Anna said, as she stood and opened her arms for a hug. "Best of luck with your move."

We always ended our sessions with a hug. I would miss that moment of intimacy, so rare in my life now.

"Thanks for everything, Anna. Take care."

How did she know I have been holding back?

I would need to go for a run when I got home.

CHAPTER 4

MEETING THE LADY

A few days after Danny told me about the first dare and the Bronze Lady, we puttered down the Hudson River in a small powerboat that Danny had borrowed from his Uncle Jimmy.

"Now, you two be careful out there. No hanky-panky," Uncle Jimmy said as he handed the keys to Danny. "Don't want to fish anyone out of the water." He smiled and I turned away as I could feel my face turn beet red.

"Sure thing, Uncle Jimmy," Danny said.

The sun shone bright in the sky as Danny fired up the engine. The boat was docked in the Tarrytown Boat Club, a marina very close to the Tappan Zee Bridge, which connected Tarrytown to Nyack. Since Danny had grown up here, I felt his excitement as he almost burst to share with me what he knew about the Hudson.

"I think the best part of the towns is the river. It's amazing! The Indians came up this river. Think about that! Then the Dutch came. Look, there's the Tarrytown Lighthouse! I think it was built in the 1880s."

We rode over closer to see it and Danny turned off the motor. "Can you imagine that families actually lived in there?" he said. "I can't decide if that would be cool or not. Awfully cramped."

He leaned over to kiss me.

How perfect is my life right now?

I placed my hands on each side of his face and kissed him back. Then I leaned back in my seat and sighed deeply.

"I am so relaxed," I said, "and so happy right now."

Danny flashed those dimples. "And I'm so glad you are," he said.

"OK," Danny said. "Let's head to the middle and head back down the river. I've got some mansions to show you!"

Danny turned the boat around and picked up speed.

"I love it when the wind whips through my hair!" I yelled.

"Yeah, me too!" Danny slowed down the boat and pointed to the shore.

"Up there is the Rockefeller mansion," Danny pointed. "My grandfather did carpentry work in the library."

"Really? Your grandfather must have been really good. Have you ever seen the work there?"

"No. It's a private home and I can't see me getting invited to dinner anytime soon."

That made me laugh out loud.

"Wow," I said. "I can't believe all the beautiful mansions we can see out here! I never would have thought."

"Yeah," said Danny.

"Look at the castle up on the hill!" Danny pointed. I looked and gasped. It was a real castle.

"Oh, that's impressive," I said.

"You know Chester from school? He knows a lot about history and he gave a report in junior high about the castle. Said that it's Irish-style, kind of medieval. The son of a Civil War general lived there."

"Danny, this is so much fun. Can you get the boat every day this summer?"

"Sure. I'll see what I can do." He gave me one of his charming winks.

After a few minutes of enjoying the view, I asked, "Danny, can you tell me about the second dare to the Bronze Lady with Jake and Timmy? You didn't get to tell me the story."

Danny furrowed his brow and said, "Yeah. Guess so."

He started his story by relating how he first met Jake in freshman year.

"We clicked right away. He played football and just fit in with all the guys," Danny said. "And Nessa." He smiled at me and raised his eyebrows.

"We were at Malandrino's eating a wedge one Saturday and he asked what there was to do in town. Timmy was with us, as always." Danny shook his head.

"Anyway, I told them about the Bronze Lady and that first dare with my friend and how we were going to go back but they moved so we didn't."

"Then Jake said, 'Maybe we should do it. Sounds cool.'"

"Before I could answer, Timmy jumped up and said, 'Yeah, let's do it! Let's do it!'"

I interrupted his story. "I can't believe you went back."

"Yeah, about two weeks later," Danny said. "This time, I ended up tripping through the wet undergrowth from the summer! Guess I deserved that for laughing at my brother.

"Carrie, even though I had seen her before, I took a really good look this time," said Danny. "The statue sits in a little courtyard almost hidden from the dirt road by two large rocks and overgrown bushes. She was as creepy as I remembered with those huge hands and arms. Weird for a lady. So big and dark and facing one of those crypts. She had cobwebs and dirt all over her.

"Timmy was the first to say something. He kept asking why she was sitting and what the hell she was waiting for. He's such a bonehead."

I nodded my head in agreement.

"Jake raided his parents' bar and brought a bottle of scotch in a paper bag for us to enjoy to celebrate our dare," Danny said.

"Timmy grabbed it first and took two long drinks. Jake knocked into him, grabbed the paper bag out of his hand and sat down on the ground.

"We were just sitting there and Jake asked again about the legend. So I told them and Timmy jumped up and spit on her!"

"What?" I asked.

"We asked him what the hell he was doing and Timmy said it was stupid to be scared by the legend. I told him *he* was stupid.

"We all kind of waited for something bad to happen after that, even Timmy though he wouldn't admit it," said Danny. "I think we all felt a little brave from the scotch so we just stayed and listened to the quiet."

"Oh my God. How creepy," I said. "I can't believe you didn't leave."

"We were trying to act all brave and stuff," Danny said. "After about fifteen minutes, I heard some rustling behind the crypt."

My mouth hung open.

"I told the guys that I heard something. I took off by myself, leaving Jake and Timmy behind. They didn't catch me 'til they got to the stone wall."

"What did you hear?" I asked, leaning towards him.

"Something just felt weird, Carrie, and I had to get out of there. I told the guys to remember to be quiet when we got back to the house. Especially Timmy."

"Wow," I said as Danny turned the boat toward the marina. "I wonder about the noise. Probably a raccoon or something."

"Yep, probably."

We were drifting now on the river. Light airy clouds were forming. I felt Danny's hand on my arm.

"Carrie? Earth to Carrie! Time to call it a day."

"Oh, yeah," I said. "Just daydreaming."

The Bronze Lady sounded fascinating.

Our high school art teacher, Mr. Caivano, told us that our after-school art club would be going on a field trip to the cemetery to sketch.

"I want you to choose something that catches your interest," he instructed us before we headed out. "It can be realistic or abstract. But remember, you want to try to marry your own vision and your own creativity with the techniques you are learning here. Anyone who wants to share can do so at our next meeting."

I was familiar with the front of the cemetery where my family had a plot and the historical graves by the Old Dutch Church, but not with the northern section. I followed some classmates as they walked and murmured about the impressive crypts and occasionally frightening statues, some of them stopping to sketch. I continued to walk alone and caught a glimpse of a huge mound of rocks on my right and some well-placed bushes. I walked into a little area, almost like a courtyard, with a very old crypt. The crypt, made from limestone, exhibited a woven stone band of leaves around the top. Underneath, I read the name, *Thomas*.

I knew I had found her. The Bronze Lady.

Facing the crypt, a bronze figure sat in an oversized chair, her ample body shrouded in a cloak. The statue towered over me, about eight feet tall and five feet wide, and was framed by tall pine trees. What drew me to her were her features. Enormous hands that should belong to a man. Large, overdeveloped forearms coming out from a woman's average-sized body, healthy and supple. Unusually long toes peeking out from under her dress just added to my interest. The chair was hard and cold, exposed to the elements. Dirt and grime had settled in the crevices of her chair and her wrap from a lack of attention. She was doomed to an eternity sitting watch over her lost soldier in this place of death.

I only had an hour to sketch before the club went back to school. After working on it all week, I shared the drawing at our club's next meeting.

"Ah. The Bronze Lady," said Mr. Caivano, walking around to my seat and picking up my work. "Isn't she amazing? What a great idea to sketch her, Carrie. Let's see what you did."

"I couldn't stop staring at her and had to remind myself to sketch," I said. "Why did the artist present her like that?"

"The title of the piece is *Recuillment*, or *Grief*," Mr. Caivano said. "The sculptor, Andrew O'Connor, Jr., was commissioned by a Civil War general's widow in the early 1900s. We know that the artist's muse was his lover but other works by him are not as bold. Any ideas on why he would sculpt the limbs like that?"

"Could he just imagine the widow's grief was over the top?" I asked.

"I don't think we will ever know," said a senior, "but could he have made the limbs larger than life to show that she represented taking on the grief of the world? I read that somewhere."

"That is very thoughtful. I appreciate the insight," Mr. Caivano said.

I felt even more connected to the Lady. Danny had been right. She turned out to be something else.

Danny, Jake, and Timmy continued to go to the Bronze Lady almost every weekend. Nessa and I went once but I didn't feel comfortable because Timmy was always there. One Sunday afternoon, Danny and I were studying at his house and decided to take a study break.

"So last night was really different," Danny said. "Chester showed up at the Lady when we were there."

"Chester? How strange," I said. "I hope you guys were nice to him."

"Timmy was a pain in the ass, of course. Jake told him to shut up."

"Did he just join you?" I asked. "What happened?"

"He said he always comes to the cemetery just to hang out." Danny shook his head, as his eyes grew really big. "That's not too strange. Anyway, he started talking about the Bronze Lady and the guy in the crypt. Chester sure is smart."

"What stuff did he tell you?" I asked.

Danny thought for a minute. "He said the cemetery was established in 1849. It's over ninety acres right now. Washington Irving made the cemetery famous, of course, in the Legend of Sleepy Hollow."

"I remember that. My father read that to me when I was about ten."

"Cool," Danny said. "Irving was a little pissed that it was originally named Tarrytown Cemetery but then, after he died, the town changed it to Sleepy Hollow Cemetery."

"Wow. Chester is so interesting."

"Then he told us something else I never even thought of," Danny remembered. "Chester told us that the Old Dutch Church and its churchyard with all those super old graves are not part of the big cemetery. Who knows that?"

"Chester's officially amazing. How long did he stay?" I asked.

"He left when we left. He said he'd look for us next time and tell us more stuff about the cemetery. He told us a spooky tale about the Lady."

"What's that?"

"Chester reminded me about the legend that anyone who knocks three times on the door of the crypt would have bad dreams that night. Of course, Timmy jumped up and did it. I hope he had nightmares."

"I'm glad you didn't test it out!" I said, laughing.

"Let's get back to work," he said, leaning over to kiss me.

You give the best kisses, Danny.

CHAPTER 5

TROUBLE'S BREWING

In July of 1989, I locked up and left my house of fifteen years in Plattsburgh to return to my family home in Sleepy Hollow. The Plattsburgh house sold quickly to a young family with a little girl. I gave my key and a warm handshake to my realtor.

Nessa took the Greyhound bus up to Plattsburgh to ride home with me. Nessa wanted to drive because she said she never had the chance to drive anywhere except around the villages. It felt odd riding in the passenger seat of my own car. We didn't speak for the first hour. Instead, we sang along with the radio. Nessa could get very spirited, jabbing her pointer finger in the air.

I'm not sure what Nessa thought about as she drove, but I thought about the many reasons why I left Sleepy Hollow in the first place. I actually love the Hudson Valley but my life there proved more complicated than it needed to be. Maybe this could be a chance for a new beginning in a familiar place. I tried to put Danny out of my mind. The idea that Nessa didn't think he stayed in town helped to temper my panic. At the same time, I couldn't help but wonder where he had been for twenty years and what he had been doing. I could feel my brow start to furrow when Nessa interrupted my thoughts.

"So, do you think you will stay in that house? A lot of people have been asking about you. Chester has been especially interested." Nessa turned to smile at me.

"Oh, great," I said. "I have no idea. I guess I'll see how I feel when I'm actually in the place. I still can't believe it, Nessa. I actually thought about my mother on my run right before the police came to my house. I wonder if she kind of said goodbye to me."

"Wow. I believe in all that, you know. I've seen too much stuff not to."

I glanced over at my friend. We had kept in contact with occasional phone calls since high school and spent time during my short visits home but I hadn't heard much about her life now. It seemed like no time had passed and we easily slipped back into the banter of high school.

"Nessa, tell me about becoming one of the first female detectives in the state. That must be amazing. Your father must have freaked out."

"My father couldn't believe it because we never talked about it. Being a cop himself, he bragged to all his buddies. I couldn't believe they even let me take the test for detective. It's not easy, though. I constantly feel like I have to do a better job than the guys in the unit. It sucks but I love getting the bad guys."

The bad guys. I tried not to cringe at those words.

Nessa talked on about her job and I let myself settle into the seat. My back started to ache and I hadn't realized how rigidly I had been sitting. I relaxed thinking about waking up every morning to a view of a beautiful river.

Sooner than I expected, we crossed the Hudson River on the Tappan Zee Bridge, and drove north on Route 9 through Tarrytown and into Sleepy Hollow.

"Love this town," said Nessa. "It hasn't changed and, yet, it has. Johnny's Pizzeria is still down Main Street and the library is on Route 9. Remember when we got kicked out of the library for our fits of laughter? Who were those boys with us? Johnny and Robert?"

We both giggled at the memory.

"I wish you had grown up here, Carrie, instead of getting here your last year of high school. You wouldn't have wanted to leave. The parades on the Fourth of July and Memorial Day were so much fun, people throwing candy to the kids and everyone marching. I joined Girl Scouts with my friends and we always had parties after the parade. And, oh my God, swimming in Kingsland Point. Amazing!"

"Nessa, you sound like you're gushing. Are you up to something?"

"What?" she said, looking at me sideways. "I would never do anything so sneaky."

At that, we burst out laughing. I had to admit, it felt good.

"Mija, what can I help you with? Are you OK?"

"Well, that came out of the blue, Nessa." It took me a few minutes to process that question.

"You can help me get over the guilt that I never came home," I said. "I made it so hard for my parents to see me, for God's sake."

"Yeah, what the hell? Why didn't you come home more except just the holidays?"

"It's complicated. My family was not like your family, in any shape or form," I said. "There always seemed to be a lot of tension in the house. But now I'm moving on and need to decide what I'm going to do here. My parents left me some money so I can take my time deciding. Want to help me?"

"You know I will."

We passed Sleepy Hollow Cemetery on the right and my mind jolted back to reality as we turned left into Philips Manor. The forsythia blooming in neighbors' yards and the beautiful purple-hued lilacs wafted welcoming scents.

When we pulled into the driveway of my parents' home, I climbed out of the car expecting to see them. But then I remembered that they were gone. There stood my home to do with as I pleased.

Something else to worry about.

I learned very quickly that moving into someone else's home is not easy. Even though I had lived here and knew in which cabinet to look for cups and glasses, plates, and spaghetti bowls, I had never realized how fastidious my mother kept her kitchen. *Her* kitchen. One of the first projects to do in the house? Make it *my* kitchen.

I drove to the local hardware store and found a treasure trove. I spent an hour looking at all the doodads and had to pick up a basket, then a cart, to hold all my goodies. Before making a final decision about contact paper, I heard my name.

"Carrie? Is that you?"

I turned to see Chester quickly approaching me from the other end of the aisle. "Oh, hi Chester."

He looked into my cart. "Getting things for your house? Nessa said you moved back. I'll bet it's really hard to make such a big change. Are—"

"Whoa!" I laughed. "Take a breath, Chester. It's nice to see you."

He lowered his head to look at the floor. *Oh, I embarrassed him.*

I reached out to touch his arm. "Yes. I'm back," I said. "Not sure if I'll stay but I'm here for the time being."

"Are you going to find a job?"

"Not right away." I stepped back to look up at his face. "Chester, I wanted to thank you for coming to my parents' funeral. I appreciate your thoughtfulness."

He nodded with a grim expression.

I grabbed some random colorful contact paper and said, "I'd better get going, Chester. Thanks again. See you around."

"Oh, bye Carrie. Hope to see you."

Driving home, I realized I would probably have to either be happy with the contact paper chosen or return it to the store. I decided to make it work and get started.

I emptied all the cabinets, put down the contact paper on the shelves, and reorganized everything to suit me. I would donate the food I would never eat to St. Theresa's Church, along with dishes and silverware. I would buy all new things for my new life. This felt good and gave me confidence to tackle the rest of the house.

I decided to do a project a day. My mother's desk, a wooden roll top secretary desk made of mahogany, always intrigued me. I coveted that piece of furniture as a child because of its wonderful wooden slots and numerous tiny drawers that could hold lots of little treasures. The roll top also had a lock with a key which my mother did not use but intrigued me enough to wonder why Mother might ever want to lock it. It never crossed my mind to get rid of this piece of my past.

Mother had always been the house manager and, as such, took care of the money, even when my father took early retirement. Interesting though that she seemed to have no awareness of the size of my father's bonuses. He must have given her just enough for her to trust him.

My father discovered a surprising passion for gardening so he dominated the outside and all that involved. He put in a Parisienne two-tier fountain in the back yard, made of concrete with ornate scrolling around the base. Each of the tiers used lion heads to spit out the water. The paperwork said it measured sixty-four inches high by eighty-three inches wide. Over two thousand pounds. Quite ostentatious. I wrote on my list that I needed to contact a landscaper to maintain the property. The list was getting long.

Taking a big gulp of my coffee, I sat down at Mother's desk to look through the massive pile of mail that had come since their death. The amount of junk mail appalled me. Apparently, if you had money, you received a lot of junk mail. As I dropped a pamphlet for new roofing into the trash basket, a lone card fell out onto the floor.

I bent over to pick it up and would have thrown it away but my name jumped out at me. Addressed to my parents, and written in block letters, it said:

> "DEAR MR. AND MRS. PETERS,
> DID YOU ASK
> CAROLYN ABOUT HER PAST?"

I dropped the card onto the desk and threw my hands up to cover my mouth.

"Oh my God!" My screams got progressively louder as I pushed myself away from the desk and started to pace around the house.

"Who sent this? Who the hell sent this?" I yelled to the ceiling as my chest began to tighten. Closing my eyes and tenting my hands over my nose and mouth, I started to inhale deeply through my nose and exhale through my mouth. About ten minutes later, my breathing returned to normal. I wanted to be done at the desk for the day but I knew I had to deal with the postcard.

I turned it over. The postmark read Albany, NY, upstate about a two-hour drive, dated January 2, 1989. I didn't really know anyone in Albany. Of course, there were people who knew me in college who might live there. But why would they send something like this? Danny and I lived a fairly low-key life in Plattsburgh with a very small group of friends. I didn't keep in contact with any of them and, although I stayed in Plattsburgh after Danny left, my social life was basically nil. I lived a solitary existence.

"This doesn't make sense!" I screamed again at the ceiling. I ran to the door to put on my sneakers and went for a run. A long one. The post card distracted me and I stepped in numerous puddles from the rain that morning. My feet and legs were soaked when I got home and, unfortunately, I didn't feel any better.

Who knew about my past?

A few days later, Nessa and I wandered around the edge of the Rockefeller Estate, up the hill and east of Sleepy Hollow. She liked to get away from the villages where she frequently ran into people she didn't necessarily want to see, like people she had arrested or had talked down from a provocation.

The Rockefeller Estate, known as Kykuit and built in 1902 by John D. Rockefeller, served as the private home to four generations of the family. We stopped at a standing plaque and read that *Kykuit* means "high point" in Dutch.

"I can't imagine living in a place like this," said Nessa.

"I know," I said. "It's honestly so gorgeous with the sparkling water, the hills, and all the trees. My parents' view is similar but this is magnificent."

We let our eyes wander, and I was reminded of something.

"Hey, Nessa," I said. "Remember after I first moved here and your Papi told the story about his Trouble Tree? I feel like I am definitely going to have to get me one of those."

Nessa's father, Fernando, became a police officer right out of high school. I remember being at their home for dinner once when a visiting neighbor asked him how he dealt with such bad people all the time. I saw him smile at Nessa's mom and she nodded back.

"Oh, I leave all my troubles outside and don't bring them into the house. Then I can just enjoy my family and friends," he said as he gestured around the room.

"That sounds good," the neighbor said, "but I can't just do that. And my job is certainly nowhere as stressful as yours."

"Did you notice the large maple tree in front of the house?"

"Sure, we have one too."

"That is my Trouble Tree," Nando said. "Every night when I come home, I place both my hands on the Trouble Tree and say a little prayer that we will have a peaceful night. It works for me!"

"What?" Nessa said, bringing me back to the present. "Why do you need a Trouble Tree? What's going on?"

I glanced away, looking at the shining water from the brilliant sun, and realized Nessa could never know my apprehension about the postcard.

"You know how I went to the will reading with my Uncle Frank? Apparently, my father included someone else as a beneficiary."

Nessa tilted her head and stared at me. "Who else would be included in your parents' will?"

"Stephanie Conway."

"Who the hell is she?" Nessa asked, her brows furrowed and mouth puckered.

"Well, this is a shocker and it's taken me a while to absorb it. Stephanie's my half-sister."

"What? You are kidding me!" Nessa stopped to sit down on the stone wall that bordered the property.

"I wish I were. She came into the meeting a few minutes after we started."

"Tell me everything," said Nessa, patting the stone next to her for me to sit down.

I told her about first seeing Stephanie in the waiting room, how Uncle Frank had told me about her existence, and then actually meeting her.

"She walked into the office and never looked at me. So rude," I said. "She's about fifteen years younger than I am. Her mother worked as my father's secretary. So cliche, it's pathetic."

"Oh, Mija. I'm so sorry. What the hell? Does she want a relationship with you? Do you want one with her?"

"She definitely doesn't want one with me, that's for sure. She is also probably going to contest the will. Apparently, the money and the boat weren't enough."

"What? Your father had a boat?"

"He had a boat with them. And, it's at the Westerly Marina in Ossining. How about that?"

"Wow. He had big cojones," said Nessa.

"Like I said, Stephanie barely even looked at me. I don't get it."

"Remember, she spent all her years without a father figure," Nessa said. "Then she finds out she has a sister who didn't."

I thought about that for a moment. "It's not my fault. It's my father's and her mother's fault. No?"

"Yes, but you probably remind her of that. Maybe she'll eventually come around," Nessa said.

"I hope she changes her mind before I die." I glanced at Nessa and we laughed. "I'd like to know what she really thought about my father, besides him being a sleaze. That would be interesting."

"She said your father was sleazy?" said Nessa. "I have to admit that I'm glad I didn't find that out about my Papi."

"What freaks me out is that they continued their affair even after our move to Sleepy Hollow. That's the reason we moved. The big scandal. How that must have hurt my mother, if she knew. She had to know, right?"

"No idea," Nessa said. "But I feel bad for her. No one should have to live with that," Nessa said.

"It's weird. Now that I found a sister, I kind of want one. Just not her. Want to be my sister?"

"Sure! Aren't we already?"

We linked arms and walked toward the parking lot to drive home.

I soon realized the idea of a project a day had been an ambitious goal and decided to work when the mood struck me. I devoted time to clearing out my parents' closets. Before donating anything, I asked Nessa to visit me at the house. She stopped by on her lunch hour for a ham and cheese sandwich waiting for her on the kitchen table. But I asked her to bring her lunch to my parents' room.

"Sure, Mija. What's up?" she asked, walking up the stairs carrying her plate.

"I want to do a fashion show for you, or actually your parents. Before I donate any of my parents' clothes, I wanted to give you a chance to bring anything to your family. If they don't want it, maybe they know family or friends who might."

"Great idea. I also know a family of five who just lost everything in a fire last week."

I brought out everything from my mother's closet first. I guess I hadn't noticed but my mother had beautiful clothes, some designer blouses and dresses. One of her Chanel suits, pink with black trim, reminded me of the suit Jackie Kennedy wore when JFK was assassinated.

"Would your Abuela want this?" I laughed as I held up the pink outfit.

"I don't think anyone in my family would wear that!" Nessa said. "But I bet you could sell it at a consignment shop in White Plains."

"Oh, I don't need the money."

"Then donate the money. Same thing, right?"

I thought about that for a moment. "That is a great idea," I said. "I'm sure Mother wore this at her country club events, not food shopping in Sleepy Hollow."

"However, I do know people who could use those winter coats and sweaters," Nessa said. "Can you drop them off this weekend at my house?"

"Sure."

Nessa glanced at her watch and said, "Gotta go!"

"Thanks for your help," I said, hugging her.

As Nessa left for the rest of her shift, I felt a little lighter. I looked up the phone number for the consignment store in White Plains. The owner said she would be happy to see my items, specifically the Chanel suit and the jewelry that accompanied it.

I could no longer avoid my mother's desk. I decided I needed to tackle the pile of mail building up again. As much as it scared me to find another postcard, I needed to get myself into a regular routine. I decided to reconcile my mother's checking account with the returned checks. As I looked over the ledger, I noticed numerous payments of $1,000.00 to a Vernon Jones.

Who is this guy?

I found a red pen in the desk drawer and started checking her past ledgers. I marked every time I saw the name, *Vernon Jones.* The checks went back fifteen years with no explanation. I looked in the bottom drawer of the desk and pulled out the phone directory for the county. I found five entries for Vernon Jones. One caught my eye right away: Vernon Jones, Private Investigator, White Plains.

Whoa. This is getting interesting. I wonder…

I called the number, not really knowing what to say. I wasn't ready when I heard, "Hello! Vernon Jones, Private Investigator. How can I help you today?"

"Uh, uh—"

"Come on, lady. Spit it out."

"OK," I said. "My name is Carolyn Peters and I found your name in my mother's check ledger. Her name was Marjorie Peters from Sleepy Hollow. She and my father were killed in a car accident in the beginning of this year. Do you recognize that name?"

"You say Marjorie is deceased?" Vernon said.

"Yes, and I'm her only child," I said. "Just trying to tie up loose ends. Can you tell me why she was sending you checks for $1,000.00 six times a year?"

"I'm afraid that's confidential. I will need to confirm her death before I speak with you."

Trying not to sound too desperate, I said, "Will you call me when you do? I would appreciate it."

"Yes," he said. "I can do that. It might be next week."

"That would be fine. Thank you very much."

I hung up the phone; my head was spinning. Did my mother know about Stephanie or was it something else?

Please call me back soon, Vernon.

CHAPTER 6

MAGICAL MOMENTS

My family's tradition during the Christmas season centered around driving to New York City and seeing all the wonders of the season. This year, my parents allowed me to bring a friend.

"Whom would you like to bring, Carolyn?" Mother said. "Nessa?"

"I want to invite Danny."

I saw the glance that passed between my parents. Father said, "We hoped you would bring Nessa. She has probably never had the experience of New York during the holiday season. Right?"

"Right. But neither has Danny. I'm going to invite him."

I surprised myself with my defiance. *You're going to spend time with him if it kills you.*

Putting on her best face, my mother said, "Please tell Danny he will need to wear a tie and jacket. We're going to dine at Luchow's after viewing the holiday displays."

"I will," I said, excited that I got my way. "I'm going to call him right now."

When I told Danny, his voice sounded a bit shaky.

"Uh, great, Carrie," he said. "I, um, just need to check with my parents. What do they serve at that restaurant? Did you say German food? Never had that before."

"Yes, they serve wienerschnitzel and funny stuff like that. But they also offer turkey and roast beef. It's a super old restaurant and kind of cool inside. And…" I paused for effect. "They can't wait to spend time with you."

"Wow. Really? I'll let you know when I talk to Ma. Thanks."

Sitting in the back seat of my parents' Cadillac, riding into New York City, I glanced sideways at Danny. He looked so handsome dressed in a tie and jacket. I smiled watching him pull his collar away from his neck. I knew he probably felt uncomfortable. He grasped my hand a little tighter when my father started talking to him.

"Danny," he said, "what are you most looking forward to seeing today?"

"I think the Radio City Christmas Spectacular. It's gotta be great if they say it's spectacular, right?" Danny smiled at me.

"Yes, I think it will be," Father laughed. "How about you, Carolyn?"

"If it's not too crowded, I hope Danny and I get to ice skate at Rockefeller Center."

Danny looked at me and nodded.

"And, you, Marjorie?" Father asked.

"I have to agree with Danny about Radio City."

Danny squeezed my hand.

"Well," Father said. "I'm looking forward to dinner at Luchow's. Danny, I hope Carolyn told you to wear comfortable shoes. We're going to do a lot of walking."

"Yes, sir. She did. Looking forward to it."

As he did every year, Father parked by Bergdorf Goodman's and Tiffany's, on Fifth Avenue and 57th Street. We zipped our jackets against the crisp winter day with a gray sky and temperature in the low forties. It took only a few minutes to walk to St. Patrick's Cathedral. My mother lit a candle in memory of her sister and parents while Danny and I visited the gift shop. Danny purchased a rosary and postcard for his mother's Christmas present. His thoughtfulness surprised me. I made sure to tell my parents.

"How lovely, Danny," said Mother.

Father nodded. "I'm sure she will be very pleased."

Danny thanked them, slightly shaking his head when he glanced at me. I think he knew why I told them. Then he smiled and grabbed my hand again.

We could see the brilliant lights and sparkling colors of the Rockefeller Center Christmas Tree before we crossed the street.

"That is amazing!" said Danny. "I have never seen anything like that before. I wish my ma could see it."

"I read in the paper," said Mother, "that the display in the tree includes statues with candelabras on their heads. Can you imagine?"

"No!" Danny and I answered at the same time.

It was a forty-minute wait to ice skate so we decided to head to Radio City for the matinee. During the walk, I sighed with relief knowing how much Danny's presence calmed me down around my parents. *I hope you never leave me, Danny.* I reached over with my empty hand to stroke his arm but my father was already talking about the history of Radio City.

"This music hall was built to be a beautiful place for the people," he said. "The developers wanted high-quality entertainment at prices ordinary people could afford. And, here we are!"

I almost choked. *Ordinary people?*

But Danny was wide-eyed as we wandered through the lobby. After the show, Danny raved about the Rockettes when we stopped to buy hot chocolate for the walk to Macy's at Herald Square to see the displays. Danny told my parents how much he appreciated the chance to see New York at such a special time. My parents smiled and Father patted him on the back.

After Macy's, Father hailed a cab to drive us to Luchow's on East 14th Street. Luchow's opened in the 1890s, served many celebrities over the years and boasted a huge Beer Garden in the back. Father loved the restaurant and the atmosphere of old Europe.

Danny didn't know where to look—at the huge ship or the twenty mounted deer heads adorning the walls. Waiters in black suits and bow ties bustled seamlessly around the tables checking in with their customers and refilling water glasses.

Reading over the special Christmas menu made our stomachs growl. Father ordered shrimp cocktails and marinated herring as table appetizers. Danny and I both ordered the roasted young Vermont turkey with chestnut dressing and fresh cranberry compote. Mother ordered roast prime rib of beef and Father couldn't wait to bite into his order of Wienerschnitzel.

"This has been such an amazing day," Danny said. "I have really enjoyed getting to know both of you, Mr. and Mrs. Peters."

I squeezed his hand under the table.

"Carrie knows my family because we spend a lot of time in Clooney's. So this has been really nice. Thank you."

My parents looked surprised and touched by his words. Father leaned over to pat Danny on his shoulder again and Mother said, "That's very sweet, Danny. We are glad you were able to come with us."

Danny whispered to me, "I was hoping to see Times Square today."

"We'll go another time," I whispered back.

Ten days later on New Year's Eve, Nessa, Jake, Danny, and I went out to dinner in White Plains to celebrate. Using fake IDs, we ordered drinks and were feeling quite good when we left the restaurant.

"It's only 10:30," Jake said. "What are we gonna do until midnight?"

"And where are we going to go to bring in the New Year?" said Nessa.

We all thought about that for a few minutes. I broke the silence.

"I have a crazy idea! Who wants to hear it?"

They all nodded in anticipation.

"We should go see the ball drop at Times Square!"

"What?" Nessa said. "I don't think we should drive into the city."

"Why can't we take the train?" I asked. "We can park at the Tarrytown station and get off at Times Square. Watch the ball drop and get back on the train to come home. Please, Danny! Please." I hugged him as I jumped up and down.

Danny looked at Jake, Jake looked at Nessa, and they all looked at me. "Yes!" said Danny. "I've always wanted to see Times Square."

We boarded the train just before it left the station and bought our tickets from the conductor. Nessa and I giggled the whole time. We arrived in New York City at 11:54 pm and could hear the crowd as we ran up the stairs. I couldn't believe our luck when we reached the street. By just stepping onto the sidewalk, we could see the glittering ball as well as the lights of Time Square. We stayed right there, avoiding the crowd, and Nessa and I snuggled with our guys. When the ball started to drop, we all held hands and counted down. With snowflakes falling on our heads, we yelled "Happy New Year" with probably five thousand of our newest friends, kissed a long time, and then hugged each other. Reluctantly, we headed down to the subway for our ride home.

The most magical moment of my life.

By mid-April of our senior year, Danny and I had been together more than seven months. We both felt it was going to last forever, especially when Danny found out that he was accepted at State University of Plattsburgh to study chemistry. I hadn't told my parents that I had also applied there and been accepted. They wanted me to go to a private girls' school like Vassar or Smith. They were not pleased and threatened to withhold my tuition money but, without telling them about Danny, I said that Plattsburgh was known as a great teachers' college and that's where I wanted to go. Surprisingly, they finally gave in.

"This will be amazing, Danny! Just think of the parties, the new friends, and the fun we'll have. And Nessa and Jake can come up and visit us." I could hardly contain my excitement. We would both live in the dorms for the first year and then figure out how we could live together. Our parents didn't need to know. We would be five hours away. I would just have to be sure I answered the phone in the apartment so my parents would not suspect. Danny could use a pay phone to call home.

"Yes. Just great," Danny said. "It'll be so good to get out of here!"

So, we continued being the "it couple" at school. We had another chance to go out on Uncle Jimmy's boat and the conversation turned to sex before marriage, the pros and cons.

Danny knew I was highly anxious so he said, "I'm sure you know that I really want to make love to you, Carrie. Right now!"

I was a bit embarrassed and turned my eyes away.

"You are so cute," Danny said. "You can barely talk about it. But I want you to feel good about it. The last thing I want to do is make you anxious. So, what do you think?"

"What happens if I get pregnant, Danny? That would ruin everything," I said, shaking my head.

Danny grabbed my hand. "We would be so careful, Carrie. I don't want you to get pregnant either."

"Um, um…I guess I want to, Danny. I can't imagine loving anyone like I love you. But I always hoped it would be special. Not in the back seat of the car."

Danny smiled. "Well, let's make it special. Leave it to me."

That little talk definitely lifted Danny's mood and he talked all the way until he dropped me off at home. I had other things to think about. Should I buy new underwear? Should I tell Nessa?

I did buy new underwear but I didn't tell Nessa. Nessa and Jake were dating, although not as seriously as Danny and me. Besides, I didn't even know if it would happen. But it was very hard not to think about it. Every time Danny and I had a date I wondered if it was that night. My nails were a mess and I had bandages on two fingers. Not very romantic.

Even Nessa noticed. "What is this?" she said as she lifted my hand to look. "Worse than normal, Mija. Are you OK?"

"Yeah. Just a lot of stuff, you know. School, college, adorable boyfriend."

"Everything all right with Danny?"

"Oh, yeah, perfect." I smiled.

Danny called me on a Saturday afternoon and said he'd pick me up for a "special night" at 5:30 PM. Before the doorbell rang, I paced in my room avoiding my parents as much as possible. When I heard him talking with them downstairs, I tried to act casual but couldn't wait to get out the door. After our trip to the city, my parents liked Danny. They thought he was a good kid, but figured I would get over him when I went to college. Even without them saying so, I knew they wanted me to marry someone from a country club crowd and live happily ever after.

Danny and I drove about fifteen minutes north to the town of Briarcliff Manor and ate dinner at Squires, a restaurant that just opened the year before. They had huge hamburgers and fries, both of which Danny could never get enough. I felt like I could barely eat so I ordered a salad with chicken and ate about half of it.

My bandages were gone but I was fiercely picking at my left thumb with my left pointer finger. I didn't want it to start bleeding, but I could not control myself. Danny saw it and took my left hand in his right when he finished eating.

"Well, how about if I get the bill and we take off?" he said.

"Sure. Sounds good."

He smiled and signaled the waiter. After he paid, he stood up, helped me with my sweater and led me out the door.

My undigested dinner seemed to rise in my throat when Danny parked the car in front of the motel.

"I'll be right back with the key. You OK?"

"Sure. Sounds good." *Am I not capable of saying anything else? Calm down, Carrie. This place looks clean and at least we won't get caught in the back seat of a car.*

The next hour passed much faster than I thought. While Danny got undressed in the bathroom, I stripped down and hid under the covers, the sheet reaching up to my neck. Danny turned off the light before he snuggled in next to me.

"Don't worry, Carrie. I'll be gentle," he said.

He tried to make me feel comfortable by kissing me. I have to admit it was nice to share that intimate moment with someone I loved so much and who loved me. But my mind was in overload and so I didn't really enjoy it.

We lay in bed for another hour just snuggling and watching TV, *The Monkees* and *Batman*. In a way, it felt like we were married. We left by 11 PM; my curfew was 11:30 and Danny never brought me home late.

We went on as if nothing had happened. But I definitely felt different, suddenly more grown-up. The secrets were only starting.

CHAPTER 7

THE THING ABOUT ANXIETY

I wouldn't be totally settled back in Sleepy Hollow until I found a therapist. It was difficult to leave Anna Baker in Plattsburgh. I felt very comfortable with her and worried that it would be hard to replace her. I asked Nessa if she knew of anyone locally.

"Hmm," she said, "do you remember Rick Simms? He graduated with us. He has a practice in Tarrytown."

"No," I said. "No. Nobody from high school." I felt a shiver up my spine. "And I prefer a woman therapist, if I can find one."

"I think there's a female psychologist in Irvington," Nessa said. "I'll ask someone at the station today for her info and let you know."

I followed up on Nessa's lead and made an appointment with Nora Cormick for the following week in August. She maintained an office in an historic building, the McVickar House, in Irvington. The blue house was an imposing four stories with windows even on the lowest level. I wondered if that was a typical basement. I unlatched the front gate and climbed up twelve steps to a wide front porch. The plaque outside the door stated the house had been built in 1853. Someone had made minor restorations so it would be attractive as office spaces. A dentist, a tax accountant, and law firm also rented space in the building. I sat outside Nora's office door and completed the paperwork left on the chair.

Nora greeted me warmly with a smile and handshake. I felt at ease right away. Nora wore her brown shoulder-length hair in a bob, with big brown eyes behind dark green glasses. She welcomed me into her office, decorated in pale blues and greens with a large Ficus tree by the window. I took a quick glance at her art pieces: a photo of a lovely field of daisies and a watercolor at a beach. I also noticed her degrees on the wall. I let out the breath I didn't realize I was holding.

"What an amazing building," I said. "I want to know what's in the basement."

"Ha!" Nora grinned. "I have not been down there. As far as I know, it's just used for storage."

"I see that you received your clinical psychology degree from Columbia. My uncle went there for the same degree. Much older than you though."

We both just nodded and I looked away, my lips tightly closed.

"So what brings you here today, Carolyn?"

"Please call me Carrie," I said. "I just moved back to the area and am hoping to find someone I can connect with."

"Have you been in therapy before, Carrie?" Nora said.

I remembered exactly when I first realized my anxiety was too much to handle by myself and I needed to talk with someone. The week had been stressful, full of nervous days and sleepless nights. I was driving home in Plattsburgh just past dusk from a trip to the store and the roads were well lit but a red light on my dashboard warned that I needed gas. The road was familiar to me and yet, suddenly it wasn't. I became confused at the upcoming exit. My heart quickened and my head started to throb with the sudden pulsing of blood.

Oh my God. Why don't I know which way to go?

I pulled over to the side of the road to calm down. Lots of deep breaths and counting in my head. I finally realized where

I needed to drive to get gas and then home. I felt totally over-whelmed. I called a therapist the next day.

"Yes, for about fifteen years with Anna Baker in Plattsburgh," I said and filled her in on my parents' deaths and my move back to Sleepy Hollow.

"Their deaths must have been very shocking. Do you feel you are still grieving?" she asked.

"Yes, and moving into the house has been more difficult than I imagined."

"Why, Carrie?"

I tried to find a more comfortable position in my chair. "I think it's really difficult to suddenly have to decide what gets thrown out, what I should keep, or give away. I have no siblings so it's all on me. At least no real siblings in my life. I'm not really a sentimental person but I find I am second-guessing myself all the time."

Nora nodded. "What did you mean when you said, no real siblings?"

I told her about my meeting with Stephanie and how I didn't think there would be a relationship with her.

Nora nodded. "Do you want a relationship with her?"

"I guess I haven't totally decided yet."

We reviewed and clarified my paperwork. Nora asked, "Why are you taking Zoloft?"

"I am highly anxious," I said.

"What does your anxiety look like?"

"I have anxiety attacks, bite and pick my nails," I said as I raised my hands to show her. "Sometimes, irrational thoughts. I run every day. That really helps."

"Are you uncomfortable if you don't run?" Nora asked.

"Yes, I am."

"Do you do anything else to get the energy out?"

I thought for a moment. "The other day it was storming all day so I couldn't get out. I flitted from one thing to the next and I could feel my heart beating faster and faster. I started to clean the bathroom and ended up spending five hours cleaning the whole house. I felt totally exhausted after that!"

Nora smiled and nodded her head. "I'll bet you were. I would be too. Carrie, do you remember being anxious even as a child?"

"Yes," I said. "I always felt a pressure to be perfect."

I hadn't realized that I had been pulling off little pieces of lint on my sweater. Nora noticed though. She averted her eyes.

"Did you feel you needed to be perfect for your parents?"

"Yes," I said. "And for myself. I guess I was a little hard on myself."

"Why do you say that?" Nora said.

"I wasn't satisfied unless I was first chair in band, or got all As. I told myself to work harder, be better, take control."

"What happens when you feel you can't control something?"

"I constantly doubt myself and the decisions I'm making." I continued to fuss with my sweater.

"When was your first time in therapy?" Nora said.

"Not until after college with Anna," I said. "A lot of things in my life changed. I wasn't in a relationship. Like I said, I felt the need to talk to someone. And, that's when I started to run."

Nora glanced down at her notes. "Carrie, you mentioned you have had irrational thoughts. What do they look like?"

"The control issue, trying to be perfect. I shouldn't do that stuff."

Nora nodded. "We are getting to the end of our time. I'm very glad you came in to see me, Carrie," Nora said. "Would you like to make another appointment with me next week so we can talk some more?"

"Yes. Same day, same time?" I asked.

"It's in the book. See you then." Nora stood up to open the door. I left her office with a lot on my mind but thought she might be someone with whom I could work.

As I drove home, I thought about how I hadn't told my other therapist everything even though we had worked together for over fifteen years. I wondered how much I would share with Nora.

Nessa and I spent a lot of time together but her work schedule as a detective ramped up, at least that's what I thought. She usually worked one day of the weekend so we spent the other day together but her pager, always on, often pulled her away from me. I realized I could afford to take at least a year off from work so I decided that volunteering at both Warner Library and Phelps Memorial Hospital on the children's ward would be perfect for me. Two things I love most: books and children.

The library was just as I remembered, but much smaller. It's always interesting how everything looks so much bigger as a child. As a volunteer at Warner Library, I shelved books and made suggestions to readers. Escaping into the rows and rows of shelves comforted me. My mother and I visited the library once a week, toting large stacks of books home. Reading, I think, proved a great escape for both of us and gave us something in common. My piles were filled with mysteries while my mother preferred biographies. Volunteering there also gave me access to the newest books, like *Wild Swans* for me and *Silence of the Lambs* for Nessa.

My experience at the hospital proved to be a different matter as I had very little practice and context with people and families in crisis. I found it very different from teaching; people were experiencing life and death decisions. My responsibilities at the hospital were to deliver flowers from the gift shop. I took the elevators up to the surgical recovery floor and knocked on one door, which was partially open.

"Come in," said a gruff voice.

"I have flowers for Florence Young," I announced in a cheery voice as I pushed open the door.

"Oh, my God," a young woman said. "She can't have flowers. She's on a respirator. Please leave us alone."

"Uh, so sorry," I said as I backed out of the room, still carrying the flowers.

Why didn't someone know about the respirator? How terrible for them. Will I need to check every patient before delivery?

I mentioned the problem to the gift shop manager. She apologized and said she would speak with someone who might be able to help.

I knew that Nessa faced issues of crises many times. While eating dinner at Clooney's, I broached the subject.

"How do you handle crises all the time, Nessa? I mean, I don't like having to solve everyone else's problems."

"That's just how I look at it, I guess. I just go into problem solving mode and take the emotion out of it until later."

"Later?"

"Yeah, it can be bad sometimes. But I really just try to concentrate on catching the bad guys. I look at the end, not the crisis at the time. And, I have my own Trouble Tree. It's a little oak tree in front of the house. Hey, it works for my dad, right?"

I nodded, smiling at the memory.

"Catching the bad guys," Nessa repeated nodding her head in affirmation and reaching for her pager as it buzzed.

"That damned pager," I said. "Can't believe it's going off again tonight. What is it this time?"

"10-57. Hit and run. Gotta go!"

Mr. Clooney put the phone on the bar so Nessa could call in. Then, she ran out the door.

I sat at the bar to talk with Mr. Clooney.

"So, how you doin' back here?" he asked. "Are you getting settled?"

"Pretty much," I replied.

We talked about my volunteering and, when I mentioned the hospital, I could see his eyes well up with tears.

"Oh, Mr. Clooney, I'm so sorry I upset you."

"No, not yer fault. I just haven't gotten over the last time I went to Phelps to visit Janice Benson before she passed. You remember Janice? She was Jake and Timmy's mother. Such a sad story, that family."

I couldn't believe that I had actually started that conversation. I looked behind him at the mirror on the wall and just wanted to wipe the sweat from my brow.

He grabbed a cloth to wipe down the bar, which was already gleaming.

"I mean, first they lost Timmy and Jake was sent to prison and they lost him. Before they even recover from that, Mike gets Huntington's Disease. Horrible thing, that disease. No cure, just the brain deteriorating. Nothing to do. Janice took care of him until he died. A saint, that one. I'm honestly surprised she kept it together."

"That's just terrible." I sat on my hands to hide my trembling.

"The wife spent a lot of time with her when she was sick. She talked a lot about her family and the good times they had before their lives exploded. At least she's at peace now."

Thank God that someone walked into the restaurant right then. I couldn't leave fast enough. "It's time for me to head home. Thanks for dinner," I said as I downed my cherry coke and grabbed my coat.

"But you don't have to leave yet. It's early. Something I said?" Mr. Clooney laughed.

Little did he know. Hopefully, he would never know how my secret impacted the Benson family.

CHAPTER 8

A TUMULTUOUS SPRING

Since Danny and I made love, he was especially attentive to me. It seems we snuck more glances at each other and I loved when he touched me on my arm, my waist, my neck.

But then the unthinkable happened. We were watching TV in my living room on a rainy Sunday afternoon in mid-May. My parents were out, visiting friends in Scarsdale. I finally found the courage to tell him.

"Danny, I'm late."

"For what?"

"My period is late."

"How late?"

"A week."

"That's not very long, is it?"

"I'm very regular, Danny."

"I've been very careful," he said, standing up. "I pulled out every time."

"I know. This is all new to me."

"Aw, shit, Carrie. I gotta go," he said giving me a quick kiss. "I'll call you later."

Danny didn't call that night and he basically avoided me the next morning before school started. When I did see him at lunch, he acted as if nothing had happened in front of his friends but I felt the distance. He didn't sit as close to me, he didn't hold my hand, and he gave me a quick hug as we parted.

Two days later I got my period. I couldn't wait to tell Danny. I asked him to meet me after school to walk to Douglas Park, about a half-mile away.

I started talking almost immediately. "It came, Danny. It came. I'm not pregnant."

"Oh my God. That's good news. Really good news."

"I know. I am so relieved. That would have been a mess."

"You're not kidding," said Danny. We talked about school gossip until we got to the park.

"Carrie, let's sit on the wall. We need to talk."

"Is everything OK, Danny? You look so serious."

Danny looked away and cracked his knuckles. He took a deep breath in and then blurted out, "I think we need to break up."

I just gawked at him, my head tilting and eyes furrowed. I couldn't think of anything to say.

"Carrie, you know how much I love you but this pregnancy thing scared the shit out of me. We're too young to be this serious. I can't do anything during the day. I'm always thinking about you."

I burst into tears.

"Aw, don't cry," Danny said and put his arm around me.

How could he use me like this? To get what he wanted and then throw me away?

"I just think we need to take a break. I don't want to date anyone else. I just need some space."

"Danny, we don't need to do it anymore. I need you in my life. I need you to hold and kiss. Please don't leave me. You promised!"

"I'm sorry. I don't want to hurt you." He stood up and slunk away.

I stood up and screamed, "You promised!" But he kept walking.

I stood at the wall and threw stones into the creek until I could control my sobbing. I trudged to Nessa's house instead of going home.

Alone. I'm alone.

Nessa and I had planned to go to the movies that evening.

"The Graduate?" I had asked when she made the suggestion. "Are you kidding? You don't like romances."

"It's supposed to be more of a comedy. Not a lot of mushy stuff. Want to pick me up at 5 for dinner first?"

"Sounds good."

But after the breakup, I showed up at Nessa's house at 4 PM, instead of 5. She immediately knew something was wrong when she saw the tears on my cheeks.

"Carrie, What's up?"

"He broke up with me, Nessa."

"What? Danny? Why?"

"Because we love each other too much. What the hell?"

"No. Tell me everything. You guys always look so happy together."

"I, we—" I started. "We went all the way. I thought I was pregnant and he freaked out."

Nessa covered her mouth as she inhaled deeply.

"But I'm not! I even told him we didn't have to do it anymore. I don't know how I can live without him, Nessa. I love—" I covered my eyes and my body racked with sobs.

"He'll change his mind, Carrie. I just know it. We'll stay away from them for a few days. Jake will understand."

"It doesn't make sense," I said. "Did he just use me for sex?"

"Oh, Mija. I know it must feel that way. But I don't think Danny is like that."

"He walked away when I asked him to stay. He had made up his mind when he thought I was pregnant. Was he going to just leave me with a baby?"

Nessa moved to sit down next to me and gave me a tight hug.

"There's no way you're going home looking like this," she said. "Your mother will never leave you alone. Spend the night."

"But it's a school night."

Nessa thought for a moment. "Just tell her we have to finish a project."

"OK."

"Do you want me to ask Jake to talk to Danny? Find out what's really going on?"

"I'm not sure." I stopped to think about her suggestion. "Do you think Danny would get mad at me?"

"Mija, what difference does it make? He already broke up with you. Let's ask Jake."

"OK, but tell Jake to make sure Danny doesn't think it's me that's asking."

"Let's call him right now." Nessa dialed the black phone on her desk. "Jake? Hi, it's me. Did you hear about Danny and Carrie?"

I tried to imagine Jake's response.

"Danny broke up with her," Nessa said. "I don't get it. Can you talk to Danny? I just gotta know what's going on." Nessa listened to Jake. "Yeah, give me a call later. Bye."

I looked at Nessa, hoping she could give me some answers.

"Sorry, Mija, he hasn't talked to Danny yet. He's supposed to see him later. Let's meet before school tomorrow to talk."

We missed the movie. When I called my mother, she started to protest but agreed because of the project. I snuggled into the sleeping bag on the floor, doubting I would get any sleep.

The next morning, I ran home to change. I met Nessa before school by her locker, looking and feeling like it had been a restless night. I grabbed her by her elbows, shaking her.

"What did Jake say?"

Two girls passed by in the hall, glaring and whispering. I didn't care.

"Jake said Danny told him just what he told you. That he freaked out about how serious and all-consuming it felt."

"All-consuming?" I asked. "Like I'm suffocating him? What the hell?"

"I don't think that, Mija. I think he just needs a little time to himself. That's all."

I was glad it was a Friday so I would only have to see Danny at school today. He was in a few of my classes but I did my best to stay away from him.

By Monday, it seemed that everyone in school knew about the breakup. I had decided over the weekend that I needed to take care of myself or Danny would never want to get back with me. But it was difficult to avoid the stares and whispers. Worse were the "Poor Carrie" looks directed at me in the halls and my classes.

Nessa told me it would get better and everyone would move on to something else. I didn't believe her.

Nessa and I had talked about going to prom since Christmas break. We bought our dresses early and made all the plans with the boys. When Danny and I broke up, Nessa begged me to go with another friend, Greg, so we could double with her and Jake. At first, I turned Greg down because I hoped that Danny would ask me, but then Jake told me Danny wasn't going at all. Greg promised we would have a good time. Three words could describe Greg: harmless, jock, partier. I had seen him at parties and he was always drunk. I figured I could drink and he would just leave me alone.

We did all the photos at my house in the back garden by my father's fountain and went out to dinner at Patricia Murphy's Restaurant in Yonkers with fake IDs. I ordered a Sloe Gin Fizz and, after my third, told the waiter, "Make it slowwww!" Everyone laughed and Greg leaned over to kiss me on the cheek.

At the prom, Jake was named King and Nessa, the Queen. I gushed with happiness for them both. Such good friends. Both Greg and I were on the Court, as was Danny, who was not there to celebrate. We danced, then left to go to the afterparty at another football player's house on Grove Street.

When we pulled up around midnight, I could hear the music, singing, and laughter inside the house from the sidewalk. We forced our way into a throng of sweaty writhing kids dancing. Greg took off with his buddies and after about an hour of more drinking and dancing, I could feel my body getting really tired. I decided to leave and walk home. It would be a long walk but I didn't want to talk with anyone, so I just left.

I soon realized it had not been a good idea to walk home. I stumbled and plodded through the streets of Tarrytown. One foot in front of the other. *Where are all the people? Where's my house?* It was pretty late. I think almost 2 AM.

"Hey, Carrie! Is that you?"

I turned to my left to see a dark blue car and someone yelling at me. "Do you want a ride?"

"Oh, Danny. Yes, yes, yes," I said as I climbed into the car. I laid my head back on the seat.

So glad Danny is here. Does he want to get back with me?

"I'm so happy to see you, Danny," I slurred. "I've missed you."

That was the last thing I remember until I woke up, groggy and disoriented. My head was pounding and I felt a heavy weight on my body, limiting my attempts to sit up. The hot breath on my neck was confusing but somewhat soothing.

"Mmm, Danny. I missed you so much," I mumbled.

"Not Danny."

I opened my eyes to see Timmy leering down at me. Fear rippled up my spine.

"What? Where's Danny? Get off of me!" I tried to get up but Timmy was too heavy and I was stuck with my legs spread open and my left arm pinned down against the front seat. I could feel Timmy's bare skin between my legs.

"Wow," Timmy laughed. "You are really gone. Danny was never here. You got in the car with me, little girl." I could feel my panties around my ankles. *Oh my God. What is he doing?*

"Timmy, let me go. Take me home!" I burst into tears.

"Nope. Not yet."

He pushed his way into me as I screamed and tried to wrench my body away.

"Oh, you're a fighter," he said. "I'm liking that. No one's going to hear you here."

I kept struggling and hitting his back, clawing, screaming and crying in his ear. *Why isn't Danny here to help me? Timmy, stop!*

"Well, Carrie. All done. We'll have to do that again some time," he said as he zipped up his pants.

I sobbed. *How could anyone be so cruel?*

I banged my head on the console as I reached down to pull up my pants. "Ow," I cried, putting my hand on my forehead. Timmy never even looked over to check on me.

Timmy pulled up in front of my house. He had barely stopped the car when I opened the door to escape.

"Bye, Carrie," he said. "See you on Monday."

He is the devil.

Fortunately, my parents were in bed when I got home so I went up to my room and collapsed onto my bed. I couldn't even make it to the shower. When I did later that morning, I grabbed the pumice stone that I usually used for my feet. I rubbed it all over my body until my skin was red and so raw the water hurt as it streamed on my body. I could still smell Timmy on me.

My mother knocked on the door. "Carrie, are you alright? My goodness, you've been in there for over thirty minutes."

"Yes, Mother. I'm coming out now." But I knew I would never feel clean again.

"Well, come down when you get out. I have lunch ready."

I first noticed the bruises on my arms and the back of my legs when I was in the shower. I would easily be able to cover them with clothes but everything I tried on seemed to irritate and rub against them. Although it was warm outside, I put on a long sleeve shirt with pants.

At dinner, I told my parents about how much fun we had at dinner and the prom. They were excited to hear that I had been chosen for the Prom Court. I assured them that Greg had been a gentleman and had taken care of me all night. After eating only a few bites which were hard to swallow, I was finally able to excuse myself to take a run.

My body was so sore. My legs hurt to move but I knew I had to release my pent-up emotions. I was so confused.

Why did Timmy rape me? Why did he hate me that much? I thought he was Danny's friend.

The running jarred my body so I changed to a fast walk.

Why did I get into Timmy's car? This is all my fault. I'll never forgive myself. Has he raped other girls? How would I find out? I can't ever let Danny know. He would be so disappointed in me. I can't even tell Nessa.

That was my final decision. I would tell no one, ever. I returned home and crawled back into bed.

My life had never seemed more worthless and each day felt like every other since Danny and I broke up. We saw each other at school and my heart pounded and my head felt dizzy until some-one said something to distract me. Then I went home after school and cried in my room.

"Carolyn, what is going on?" my mother said. "I can tell you are sad because of Danny, but you seem beyond sad. Will you please talk to me? I'm worried about you."

"No! No! I can't talk about it. Leave me alone!" I stomped to the front door to put on my running shoes. "And don't pre-tend you are upset we broke up. I know you and Father didn't think he was good enough." I made sure to slam the door on the way out.

I pushed my body harder than usual to try to clear my head. I ran my regular route lasting about forty minutes so I wouldn't have to think about where to go. Mother appeared at the front door to greet me when I returned.

"Carolyn, I made your favorite dish for dinner," my mother called out as I bolted upstairs. "Veal curry with rice!"

"Not hungry. I'm not hungry," I yelled.

Next thing I knew my mother knocked on my bedroom door. She didn't wait for an invitation to enter.

"Carolyn, this is out of hand. You aren't eating and I hear you in the bathroom in the middle of the night. I also received a call from school today from your English teacher. She said you seem to be having trouble concentrating. I think you should see our doctor."

"What?" I screamed. "So he can tell me I'm crazy? Get out, Mother."

I didn't see a doctor but I did have to face my English teacher the next day after school. I always felt comfortable walking into her classroom because I felt she really cared about me and my work. Today, I stared at the purple African violet on her desk.

"Carrie, I am very concerned about your work lately," Mrs. Kingston said. "Do you want to share anything with me? Maybe a different perspective would help."

"Oh, it's just high school and boyfriend stuff," I said. "Nothing I shouldn't be able to figure out."

I didn't dare look her in the eyes. I knew she'd see right through me. Then, what would happen? Would I have to miss school and get further behind? Would she tell my mother I had been raped? Would the whole school find out I had been raped? What would Danny do? He would never love or touch me again.

"Carrie." Mrs. Kingston reached out to touch my arm. "Carrie, look at me. I can tell you are getting agitated. Let's just take some deep breaths to calm down. Can you do that with me?"

I made myself look at her because I thought I would pass out at any moment.

"Breathe in 2, 3, 4...breathe out 2, 3, 4."

After about ten of those, I started to feel a bit better and I assured her I would go home to rest. I had to do better if I wanted to protect myself.

I dreaded seeing Timmy at school, fearful that he would attack me again. I knew that was unlikely in school but I couldn't stop myself. I started wearing my hair down to cover my face as I walked through school. Passing Timmy in the hallway or watching him joke around with Danny made me shiver. But he just wouldn't leave me alone.

"Hey babe. Do you miss me?" Timmy whispered in my ear with kissing noises when we passed in the hall. I gagged from his hot, smoky breath. Then he made that terrifying laugh which sent tremors up my spine.

After the last time he did that, I saw him coming toward me again in the hall and turned around to avoid him. But classes were changing, the hallways were packed, and I ended up getting pushed back in his direction. Panicking, I tried turning around again and gasped.

We were face to face when he leaned in and said, "Hey Carrie. Want to do it again?"

I guess he didn't realize that Danny and Nessa were behind him. When I burst into tears, they both came running up to me. Danny grabbed and hugged me.

"Danny, can I see you after school?" I said between my sobs, looking to see Timmy glancing back as he walked away.

As Nessa forced me to go to the Nurse's Office, I saw Danny nod his head.

Nobody knew it had been Timmy's fault. Everything was Timmy's fault.

But there were so many, many reasons to blame myself for what happened to me. I had been drinking. I decided to walk home alone. I passed out in Timmy's car.

After school, Danny met me in the Nurse's Office, where I had been all afternoon. The nurse had been nice and let me stay. No one else had needed her.

Danny and I walked to Douglas Park.

"Oh, Danny, I don't know where to start. I am just so glad to be talking with you."

"I know, Carrie. Me too," he leaned over to hug me. "What happened? I've never seen you burst into tears like that."

"I need you to listen to me all the way through," I said. I had decided to tell him about Timmy. I couldn't keep it to myself any longer.

I could feel my heart palpitations start. "Would you hold my hand?"

"Wow, it's sweaty, Carrie. Are you OK?"

"I'm better now. Danny, do you know what happened on Prom night?"

"No, I didn't go, remember? But you went with what's his face."

I had to smile. "Yes, I went with Greg. I didn't really want to but Nessa wanted me to double with her and Jake. I already had my dress. But all Greg wanted to do was drink. Before, during, and after. By the time we were at the after party at

Rigby's house, he could barely stand. I was pretty drunk too. So, I left and started to walk home. I didn't tell Greg or Nessa. Just left."

"I can't imagine how drunk you were," Danny said. "Never seen you drunk. Did you have a lot?"

"Yes. I was just kind of staggering, I think, and I heard a car stop next to me and someone ask if I wanted a ride. I thought it was you. But it was Timmy."

"So Timmy drove you home?" said Danny. "Hmm. An unnatural nice act."

"No. That's the problem."

Danny stood and started to pace. Now that I started, I had to keep going.

"Please let me finish," I said. "I have to get this all out now."

"Fine," he said as he sat back down. "Go ahead."

"So, I got into Timmy's car and laid my head back on the seat. I must have passed out because, when I woke up, I felt something touching my stomach and making noises on my neck. I brushed them away when I opened my eyes and saw Timmy on top of me."

"That fucker!" Danny yelled.

"Even worse, my dress was pushed way up and my underwear was around my ankle. Danny, he raped me. He raped me!" I burst into tears again and hid my face in his chest.

Danny jumped up again, his fists clenched at his sides.

"What you saw in school?" I continued between sobs. "Timmy has been whispering stuff in my ear when I pass him in the hall. It's terrible."

Danny picked up a rock and threw it hard against the nearest tree.

"Oh, Danny, please calm down. I'm so sorry. I shouldn't have told you."

"Calm down?" Danny said, the vein in his neck bulging. "Listen, Carrie. I didn't hear Timmy say anything to you in the hall so, when I saw you burst into tears, I just thought I didn't understand girls at all."

"I know, Danny," I said. "It's been awful without you."

"Wait til Jake hears what his brother did," Danny said. "Let's go to my house and call Jake. I'll tell him that he and Timmy need to meet me at the Lady tonight instead of tomorrow."

"I'm coming too, Danny," I said.

"OK. I guess so. Timmy has no idea what's in store for him. I feel bad that Jake will be in the middle of it."

I don't think I have ever seen Danny so mad. I didn't think I could ever forgive Timmy but I needed to get it off my mind and I felt that Danny would keep my secret. Danny seemed to calm down after a bit and we decided that he would just talk to Timmy and ask him to apologize to me and stop bothering me.

It turned out Danny just pretended to be calm.

Danny called Jake as soon as we arrived at his house. We ate a quick dinner and took a brisk walk to the cemetery. Danny didn't talk on the way but he squeezed one of my hands really tight and I could see his other fist opening and clenching. I didn't know if he would control himself when he talked to Timmy. Maybe Jake could calm him down. He seemed good at that.

But that idea fell apart when we saw Timmy sitting at the Bronze Lady alone. Already drinking, he yelled that Jake would be coming later because their mom needed him to move some chairs from the garage into the house.

"Get up!" Danny screamed as he approached. "Get up!"

"Whoa, what's with you?" Timmy said. "Carrie not giving you any?"

Danny took a deep breath and said, "You are such an asshole, Timmy! What makes you such an asshole? Why are you so mean? You are nothing like Jake."

"Right!" Timmy yelled back. "I'm nothing like Jake. I like it that way!"

"Carrie told me what you did to her. You are pathetic. Man, I thought you were my friend."

"Friend?" said Timmy. "You put up with me because I'm Jake's brother. She wanted it. Oh, yeah, she wanted it."

Danny seemed to be vibrating. It scared me to see him like that. He turned to me and said, "Sorry, Carrie."

As I reached out to him, he turned and punched Timmy in the face. Blood from his nose spurted everywhere. That was the first time I ever saw anyone punch or get punched. As Danny pulled his arm back to punch him again, I started screaming and he turned to look at me.

"Stop! Danny, stop. He's not worth it!"

Timmy pushed Danny from behind and he fell to his knees onto the grass.

"Damn it!" yelled Danny.

He scrambled to get up and didn't see Timmy approach him again. Timmy grabbed Danny's hair with his left hand, pulled up his head, twisted it around and smashed him in the chest with his right hand. I plunged forward to wedge myself in between them only to fall to the ground.

Danny, still trying to catch his breath, struggled to crawl between me and Timmy. When Timmy started back toward Danny, I grabbed Timmy's legs to pull him off-balance. He flew backwards.

At almost the same moment, I heard a loud thud and groan. I sat up to see that Timmy had hit his head on the edge of the crypt. His body went still. A puddle of blood formed on the ground.

"Oh, no," I screamed. "Danny, is he—"

"I don't know! We gotta go!"

Danny and I took off clutching each other, Danny limping and breathing hard. I turned to look back to see Timmy, at the Bronze Lady's feet, not moving.

We ran as quietly as we could through the darkening cemetery. Danny grabbed my hand to pull me along faster. I felt almost parallel to the ground. I just wanted to pick up my feet and fly away. Getting to the edge of the property, we blindly ran across Route 9 as cars blasted their horns, one barely missing my leg. We ran until we reached my house, then collapsed on the front porch.

My limbs stiffened as it seemed like electric jolts ran from head to toe and back again. I knew the difference between this and a panic attack. I felt pure unadulterated fear with the realization that we were a part of a horrible and irreversible set of events. I have heard people say that trauma will change your life. In those moments after, all I could do was fight to breathe and unsee the image of Timmy on the ground, motionless, eerily quiet. No abrasive or obnoxious comments, no leering looks. Just bleeding next to the Bronze Lady, whom he had spit upon in defiance. Bleeding to death, alone in a cemetery.

Danny put his arms tightly around me to try to stop my trembling.

"Carrie, I'm here," he whispered in my ear as I struggled to loosen his grip. "I'll stay with you."

"But what should we do, Danny? What should we do?"

We sat entwined for almost an hour, Danny whispering and rubbing my arms. I slowly felt my limbs return to normal and, bracing myself against Danny's shoulder, stood and walked into the house. I never said a word to my parents. Danny and I tried never to talk about that night again.

Not even after Jake went to jail.

CHAPTER 9

INCREASED DISQUIET

The town heard the blares of the firehouse at 3:41 AM. Still half-asleep, I ran to the list hanging by the kitchen phone. The fire departments in Tarrytown and Sleepy Hollow blasted their horns in a code to let the police and volunteer firemen know the location of the emergency. It alerted residents as well. Three blasts, pause, four blasts, pause, and then eight blasts. I quickly found the code on the list: the Tarrytown Railroad Station.

The railroad stations served as a lifeblood to the villages. Nessa told me that her family had once lived in an apartment right by the station and could hear the train whistles at night. The station itself was a one-story stone building, the outside not revealing the age of its interior, having been renovated. Running right along the Hudson River, the tracks brought commuters and visitors both into and out of New York City. Many young adults living at home traveled to colleges or trade schools in or around the city. For those young women who were not encouraged by their families to go away to college or who couldn't afford it, the train provided a way to new experiences.

I knew I would not be able to talk with Nessa until after the emergency. I turned on the television at 6 am for the morning news and listened as the reporter introduced Nessa.

"This is Detective Martinez from the Tarrytown Police Department. Can you tell us what happened?"

"A white woman, approximately seventeen to twenty-one years old, 5 feet 4 inches with short brown hair was sexually assaulted and left for dead by the railroad station in Tarrytown," I heard Nessa report. "She dragged herself out of a late model four-door Honda sedan as it started burning and collapsed about ten feet away. The flames barely missed her but she was scorched by embers. She is still unidentified. We are asking for help or leads to identify this woman. She is under police guard at the hospital. Our police chief will give a full press conference later this afternoon at 2 PM. No more questions, please. Thank you."

"Thank you, Detective Martinez. If you have any information, please contact the Tarrytown Police Department. See the number on the screen," said the reporter.

As I listened to the news, I felt lightheaded. Not that I had been burned alive in a car but I knew what it was like to feel helpless.

My thoughts went into overdrive as I sat huddled on the couch and sobbed. *I've got to protect myself. Keep people out. Everyone. Even Nessa. That's how I'll be safe.*

I awoke to pounding on the front door and Nessa threatening to break it down if I didn't open it up immediately.

"Carrie. Open up!"

"All right, all right. Just a minute," I complained, dragging my body to the door.

When I opened the door, her face reflected how I felt.

"Jesus Christ, Carrie! What is going on with you?" Nessa rushed in and hugged me. "Don't you answer your phone anymore? I've been calling since early this morning." She dragged me into the kitchen to make me some tea and toast. "I couldn't get over here sooner. I've got enough to worry about." She walked around the kitchen, jabbing her index finger in the air and cursing.

But I still couldn't tell her about the assault or Timmy. No one knew except Danny.

Nessa called later that afternoon and asked if I wanted to take a ride with her to Poughkeepsie, about two hours north, the next morning. She had to interview someone for a case. She would drop me off at the mall while she went to the interview.

"Who are you going to talk with?" I asked.

"Can't tell you specifics," Nessa said.

"Is it related to the girl in the train station?"

"Can't talk about it," Nessa said and changed the subject. "I'll pick you up at nine."

Nessa showed up right on time the next morning, September 7th. I was looking forward to a lot of Nessa time. Her pager lay nearby, even though she was off-duty.

"Glad you could keep me company, Mija," Nessa said, switching the radio station to FM. Within seconds, her body moved to the beat of a song.

"What is this song? Never heard it before," I said, feeling my head starting to bob.

"Blue Monday by New Order. I get tired of listening to Top 40. That's all my partner wants to listen to when we're on patrol. So, this is me in my off-time!"

I smiled as I watched her right shoulder move forward two beats, followed by the left two beats. Fingers of both hands drumming on the steering wheel and head bobbing as she sang along with the words. Smooth and deliberate movements but, even sitting down, mesmerizing. I always wanted to move like that. Each song more enjoyable than the last. I think I needed to reset my radio buttons.

"Hey, Nessa, have you seen Chester very much over the years since high school?"

"Yes, quite a bit. But not because he's ever been in trouble with the law." We both looked at each other and chuckled.

"Has he ever had any friends?" I asked.

"I don't know. He's always alone when I see him. If he comes into Clooney's, I always invite him to sit with me and whomever. He doesn't say much but I can tell it makes him feel good. Why all this sudden interest in Chester?" She raised her eyebrows and threw me a quizzical look.

"It's not what you're thinking, Nessa!"

"That's too bad for Chester. I think he's always had a crush on you."

"Yeah, well, that's never gonna happen." I looked out the window as we passed through Garrison, another little town on Route 9 North. "I think back to high school and he was always alone. So sad."

"Yeah. It must have sucked for him. I'll tell ya, though. He sure knows a lot about Tarrytown and Sleepy Hollow. I told him once I thought he should apply to be the historian or write a book. Especially about the cemetery. We gave him a little party at Clooney's when he got his Master's Degree in History and started his job as a museum archivist at the American Museum of Natural History in the city. Amazing, right?" Nessa glanced over at me, shaking her head. "But we found out kinda by accident. His father is friends with Mr. Clooney so he told us. You should've seen Chester's face when we celebrated him."

"That was really nice, Nessa. I can just imagine how much that meant to him."

Nessa interrupted my thoughts. "OK if I drop you off here? How about if I meet you in a couple of hours and we'll get some lunch?"

"Sounds great. Good luck with your interview."

I spent the beginning of the two hours drinking coffee and eating an oatmeal cookie. I stopped into the small, independent bookstore next door and bought a Sports Illustrated magazine for Nessa with Michael Jordan on the cover, whom she obsessed over. She still enjoyed an occasional game of pick-up basketball.

Nessa came back in a really good mood when she picked me up. We ate a delicious lunch in Poughkeepsie near Vassar College but she kept looking at her watch.

"You really want to get back, don't you?" I asked. "You're gobbling your food."

"Yeah. All I'll tell you is that it turned out to be an informative interview. We found out the victim's identity. Can't wait to get back to the station."

"Then let's not waste any more time. Let's go!"

We drove back to Sleepy Hollow, going just a few miles over the speed limit. Nessa dropped me off at home. I didn't hear from her for two days.

I think I reacted to Nessa's absence with increased anxiety. I had one of those dreams that you swear really happened.

In my dream, I busied myself in the house, bumping into people everywhere and then stopping in the living room to fold freshly laundered sheets and pillowcases. Out of the corner of my eye I saw an arm and hand picking up a pillowcase. I turned my head and saw Danny. I hadn't seen him in a long time. He asked me for a hug and then fell onto the couch and patted the spot next to him. I sat, lost in those beautiful green eyes, twinkling and inviting.

"You are too comfortable, Danny," I said.

As I leaned in to kiss him, I woke up with a start. "What the hell?"

I tried not to think about Vernon Jones but I had to admit I thought about him every single time I passed my mother's desk. Finally, he returned my call after three weeks.

"Hello, Miss Peters? This is Vernon Jones, getting back to you."

"Yes," I said. "I was hoping to hear from you."

"I checked out your mother's death. So sorry to hear that she passed. She was a classy lady."

"Thank you," I said. "Can you tell me why she was employing you?"

"I don't really feel comfortable doing that," he said.

"What if I ask you questions? Will you confirm or deny?"

"I guess I might be able to do that," Vernon said. "We can try that out."

"OK," I began. "I know my father had an affair and a daughter, whom I just met a few months ago. Did your employment concern that relationship?"

"Yes, unfortunately, it did. I am sorry you had to learn about that after their deaths."

"But, why?" I continued. "Why did she continue to pay you after she learned of the affair?"

"Your mother wanted to keep tabs on that relationship." Vernon sighed deeply. "She once told me that she felt she had some control because she knew what he was doing. I did surveillance every two months and verbally reported back to her."

"I know that you reported to her verbally but I'm wondering if you have any written reports? I can pick them up. You're in White Plains?"

"Don't bother," Vernon said. "I'll mail them tomorrow."

"Thank you again, Mr. Jones. You have been really helpful."
Wow. Mother knew.

CHAPTER 10

JUSTICE FOR TIMMY

Danny, Nessa, and I attended Timmy's wake at Coffey's Funeral Home on Broadway in Tarrytown. Jake was in the county jail, awaiting arraignment. Both Danny and Nessa had been to wakes before because of deaths in their large families. It was the first one I had ever experienced of someone our age. Approaching the casket, I grabbed Danny's hand and closed my eyes as he led me the last few steps.

"Oh, my God," I whispered, as I opened my eyes. "He looks so peaceful."

"Yeah," said Danny. "Like he's sleeping."

"Oh, Danny," I turned my head into his chest.

Just then, Mrs. Benson approached us and I felt her arm around my waist, as she appeared to comfort me.

I felt my whole body stiffen, avoiding her eyes.

Oh, God. She's comforting me. One son dead. The other in jail.

"Carrie and Danny," she said. "Thank you both for being here. Jake just loves you both so much."

"I wish he were here," Danny choked up.

"So do we, dear."

We stayed another half hour and then left with Nessa to go back to Danny's house. We talked about memories with Jake. I was so worried that Nessa would see through me.

"I felt so lucky to have Jake as my boyfriend," Nessa said. "Did you know he brought me Reese's peanut butter cups whenever he picked me up for dates?" She chuckled. "My favorite. I'll bet I gained ten pounds because of those. But I never turned them down."

"I felt lucky that Jake was my best friend," Danny said, avoiding our eyes. "I could talk to him like another brother. He had my back. One time, I didn't do my homework assignment in O'Neal's class because I was helping Pa at the bar. He let me copy his before we went to class."

"And I felt lucky that he loved both of you enough to welcome me into your circle," I said.

We didn't speak about Timmy until Nessa broke the ice.

"I hate to speak ill of the dead," she said. "But why was Timmy so mean? I didn't get it. Jake is such a sweet guy."

"Jake told me once he let Timmy hang around with us because he didn't have any other friends," said Danny. "Jake said his father asked him to include Timmy. Guess he never realized what a pain he was to Jake."

Nessa and I looked at each other and nodded. "Such a pain," said Nessa.

I grabbed a napkin. Under the table, my hangnail started to bleed.

The next day, many people in Sleepy Hollow and Tarrytown crowded into Transfiguration Church to attend the funeral service for Timmy Benson. Although the family had lived in Sleepy Hollow for only a few years, Mike and Janice Benson had quickly made friends by volunteering and entertaining in their home. I arrived first and found a seat near the back. Danny, Nessa, and Chester joined me within a few minutes.

Catholic masses last about an hour so I had a lot of time to think about what Danny and I had done and hadn't done.

Would we really be able to maintain this secret? By the end of the mass, I convinced myself that Jake would never be found guilty or go to jail. Danny and I would have to maintain the secret and live with the guilt. That was our punishment. A lifetime of guilt and secrets.

Justice for Timmy moved quickly. The trial against Jake, charged with manslaughter in Timmy's death, painted brothers at odds: Jake's successful high school experience and Timmy's often offensive personality. Jake's defense claimed that Timmy fell on his face and then fell backward and hit his head because of the drinking before Jake got to the cemetery.

Nessa, Danny, and I were character witnesses for Jake's defense and not allowed into the proceedings until we were called. The prosecutor questioned Chester on the stand and he told us after what he said.

"Chester, tell us what you saw the evening of June 2, 1967."

"I heard shouting as I approached from the other side of the cemetery. When I finally got to the Bronze Lady, I saw Jake kneeling over Timmy. Timmy was on the ground, bleeding."

"What did you do then?"

"I ran to the closest house and asked them to call the police."

We stopped at Clooney's after our appearances. Nessa, Danny and I discussed what we each had said on the stand about Jake.

Nessa said, "I said I loved him and that he was a good person. Timmy had been erratic."

Danny said, "Jake was my best friend. Timmy hung around with us but he was very different. He could explode at a minute's notice."

And I said that Jake became a kind and sweet friend, but that Timmy could be mean. I didn't mention how mean.

Danny had also been asked about his phone call to Jake to meet him that night at the Bronze Lady. "I told the defense attorney that you called me, Carrie," Danny said, "and were upset because we had broken up. So, I went to see you instead."

I nodded but couldn't meet his eyes.

We were so sure Jake would be saved because he was such a good guy. Also, Danny and I knew he was innocent and tried to convince each other that the jury would be fair and see that it was an accident.

But, despite our youthful naivete, the jury felt that Jake had motive, opportunity, and the means to kill Timmy. He had been found with Timmy's blood on his hands and clothes. Jake was convicted of involuntary manslaughter in early July and sentenced to eight years at the Ossining Correctional Facility, better known as Sing Sing, about ten miles north of Sleepy Hollow. Sing Sing is a maximum-security prison on the banks of the Hudson River. My parents talked about Sing Sing over the dinner table the night of Jake's conviction.

"The name comes from the Sintsink Native American tribe from whom the land was purchased in 1685," my father said.

Oh, my God. Who the hell cares about how it was named? I started to pick at the hangnail on my left thumb.

"I just can't imagine how Jake's parents are doing. Philip, we should ask them to dinner," said my mother.

Yes, wouldn't that be the proper thing to do? Why don't you do that, Philip and Marjorie?

"Have you ever heard the slang expression, 'going up the river?'" my father said. "That started because prisoners took a boat to get to Sing Sing."

I couldn't take listening to them anymore and my thumb was bleeding. "May I be excused?" I asked, and went for a run after getting a bandage.

I called Jake to talk at least twice a week before Danny and I left for college. I felt a tremendous amount of guilt but was not brave enough to say anything. This was my atonement. I have to admit I was glad to be leaving because I found it hard to talk with him, even harder to listen to him. He talked about how he felt like a caged animal and could not believe how his life took this turn.

"I know no one believes me, Carrie, but I just found Timmy like that. I could never kill my brother. Shit. I was almost always pissed at him but he was already laying on the ground when I got there."

"What does your lawyer say?" I asked him.

"He said that so far there's no chance for an appeal. The evidence was clear. I was the last one with Timmy. I wish Danny had been there."

"I am so sorry that Danny was with me."

"Yeah," Jake said. "That's what Danny said. But he never told me why he wanted to meet that night instead of the next."

"Danny told me he made the change and then realized that I needed to see him," I said.

Danny and I thought a lot about Jake, but never talked about the truth, even when alone. We had returned to our full relationship of codependence and sex.

"We are both cowards. I don't know how to live with this, Danny," I said, tearing up. "Please don't ever leave me, Danny. I can't live with this without you."

"I won't leave. I promise."

Danny walked me home one late summer evening after a get-together at Nessa's house. As if our lives weren't complicated enough, I had another secret to share with him.

"Danny," I said. "I'm pregnant. I thought I was late because of the stress but this time, I'm sure."

Danny stopped abruptly. "What?"

"I think I'm almost three months. But I was thinking that we'll be away at school. Can't we figure this out?"

"Whoa, Carrie. I need time to absorb this."

We walked the rest of the way in silence. At my door, Danny turned me to face him and said, "We can deal with this, Carrie. We've faced a lot worse. Right?"

I nodded and lay my head on his chest.

"Just keep it between us. OK?" he said.

I nodded again and kissed him good night.

Another huge secret.

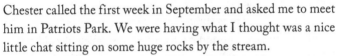

CHAPTER 11

CHESTER

Chester called the first week in September and asked me to meet him in Patriots Park. We were having what I thought was a nice little chat sitting on some huge rocks by the stream.

"I was a bit surprised that you called," I said. "How have you been?"

"OK."

"Did you go away to school?" I asked.

"I never left the area," Chester said.

"But you did go to college, right? I remember you were very smart." He was a bit difficult to engage in conversation.

"I attended college at Fordham so I could commute and live at home. It was easier that way."

"Where do you live now?" I asked.

"I still live with my father in the Pennybridge area. My mother passed away eleven years ago."

"Oh, I'm sorry, Chester. I didn't know she had been sick."

Chester looked away. "You know, Carrie, I saw you," he blurted out.

I could feel my throat constricting and my heart beating faster as I tried to keep my face calm. There was only one thing I worried about him seeing. So long ago. Still something to run from.

"What do you mean 'you saw me'? Saw me where?"

Chester just looked at me, his expressionless face giving me no clues as to where he saw me or why he even said that. Without a word, he stood up abruptly to leave, red-faced, his hands shaking.

"I thought I was ready to talk about this." He grabbed his backpack and hurried away. I reached out for his arm but he was too quick for me. I watched him walk away and I turned when I heard a group of toddlers squealing and playing in the stream nearby, closely watched by their moms. My knees wobbled as I stood. I reached back to steady myself on the rock when I noticed something on the ground behind me.

What's that? I'm sure that wasn't there when we sat down.

I bent to pick it up and it felt dusty and smelled like old coffee. The dates on the binding of the book read 1967-1968. Inside, the yellowed paper bore chicken-scratch writing that made it hard to read. But as I flipped through the pages, I clearly saw that Chester had signed each entry.

"Oh my God! This must be Chester's journal!"

I glanced around to see if he was still in the area but he was gone. Although I felt guilty for snooping, my hands shook as I opened to the first page of the journal. Pulling my eyes away from the page, I looked over my shoulder to make sure Chester had left the park.

Why did he bring this here? Would this journal give me a clue to what he saw?

I rushed home to read the journal, but kept fidgeting and couldn't get comfortable. I kept glancing at the door, expecting someone to walk in. I checked the lock on the door. Finally, I tried to settle into the couch to start reading. The entry dates were from high school. But that wasn't the only thing that surprised me.

He signed each entry, "Your best friend, Chester."

September 25, 1966

Dear Journal,

My first entry. Mrs. Kingston, my English teacher, gave us an assignment to write a journal entry every day for a week. I can write anything I am thinking about. Each one has to be at least a page long. She said she isn't going to read the entries. She will just check that they are completed. Privacy issues, she said.

I guess I'm supposed to write about how great my high school experience is but honestly, it isn't.

It's the middle of football season. That means pep rallies with cheerleaders telling us to yell and clap for the football players. I may have to go to the pep rallies but I don't ever go to the football games because I have no one to go with. And besides, on Saturdays my parents and I visit my grandmother in Irvington.

At least I have my comics. Superman comics. I used to think that maybe I had superpowers because I could see the vapors coming off the radiators in our house. I like Superman because he always wins.

I also really like the Archie comics because they are about kids in high school. Yesterday, I bought the Betty and Veronica #135. It's so funny. The guys become obsessed with drag racing and the girls try to figure out how to get them to pay attention to them. Then Veronica criticizes Archie's dancing skills so he signs up for lessons. All the dance teachers are beautiful

and Veronica gets so mad! 36 pages of laughs!
I wish I knew who else reads comic books.
Maybe that guy in my homeroom Richard or
the kid in English named Bill. Maybe I'll get
up enough nerve to ask them some day.

Your best friend,
Chester

His writings were a peek into the mind of a very lonely kid. I
flipped through a bunch of pages and continued reading.

November 4, 1966

Dear Journal,

I had the strangest dream last night. I woke
up totally tangled in my sheet and sweating in
the middle of the night. I dreamed I was in a
fast-moving river trying to stay afloat. But I
wasn't scared at all, even though I can't swim.

A large black crow flying over the river
sang to me and said, "Chester, you have a long
way to go to get to your destination. You need
to continue on your path to reach your reward.
You will not be able to stop for breaks or you
will have to start all over again on your journey."

I could see the sides of the river but seemed
to be stuck in the middle. Then the bird turned
suddenly and fell into the river and that's when
I woke up.

I wonder if the dream means anything important. I wish I understood dreams. Maybe
I'm on my way to something exciting and my

life will change. But the crow crashing into the river worries me. I hope nothing bad happens to me.

This whole water dream is really weird. I do not know how to swim and am really afraid to go into the water. A lot of the high school kids swim at Kingsland Point or Phillips Manor Club on the river but I have never even been down there. It would be too embarrassing to be seen in a bathing suit and not swim.

Your best friend,
Chester

I loved swimming at the club. Didn't this kid ever have fun? I was hooked and kept reading. I browsed quickly through a few until I saw my name and stopped to read.

December 2, 1966

Dear Journal,

I changed my walk today. Instead of walking through town, I walked up the hill to the Lakes. It's the upper part of the reservoir and I always hear the kids talking about ice skating there. That's another thing I've never done. I'd be too afraid I would fall and give people more reasons to make fun of me.

I saw Carrie there with Danny. I almost didn't recognize her because she was all bundled up. But I heard her laugh and there she was skating and holding hands with him. I watched them for a while. They laughed a lot when Timmy fell down. He got really mad and pushed Jake 'cause he blamed him. Seems like Timmy is always mad.

Anyway, I turned and walked home when I saw the kids head toward the red shed to take off their skates. I was afraid they would see me.

Your best friend,
Chester

I thought more about the journal entries on my evening run. High school had been a harsh place for Chester. I was sure of that. I saw the way the bullies bumped into him and how he sat alone at lunch or at the ends of tables so he looked like he belonged. Most kids didn't mind; they just didn't engage with him.

Chester called later that evening while I was still reading.

"Carrie? This is Chester. I lost something today. Did you find anything at the park? I really need it back. I really do."

"Uh, no," I said. "What did you lose?"

"A journal," Chester said. "I lost my journal."

"Oh. Hope you find it."

I hung up the phone quickly, feeling myself starting to hyperventilate. *Did he hear anything in my voice? Oh, what if he knows I have the journal?*

Something he said in the park nagged at me, or maybe how he said it?

What did Chester mean? I didn't think anyone saw us at the cemetery that night. I decided to read all night to finish the journal. I didn't know how long I would be able to keep it.

It was fascinating to realize that Chester was really bright but so isolated in his life. I guess he had so much time to think about everything that happened around him. Most of his entries were not very interesting but some almost read like stories.

December 18, 1966

Dear Journal,

I always wanted to be called Chet. In middle school the mean boys used to call me "No-chest Chester" so I wanted to be a different person. Maybe it was my name that was making the boys be mean to me. My dad says I should be proud of my name. Chester was my great-great grandfather's name and he lived a good life.

I had the water dream again. I wonder if it's common to have the same idea in dreams. This one was a little different since I was floating near the edge of the river and laying on tree trunks that were standing straight up but not going anywhere. I kept looking for the black crow but I didn't see him. I was hoping he would talk to me again. A bird is better than no one else.

I think I felt OK floating in the river. I didn't feel scared and I was laying on wet leaves so the branches didn't poke me. Looking up, all I could see were dark, angry clouds bumping against each other but no rain. I just remember I couldn't see the sun at all. Dreams are weird. But fascinating.

Your best friend,
Chester

I have to admit that I felt my stomach ache as I read Chester's journal. I walked into the kitchen to make a cup of tea, hoping that would help. I knew that he deserved his privacy. I knew what I was doing was wrong. But I had to find out what he had seen. If that meant I had to read his whole diary, then so be it.

June 4, 1967.

Dear Journal,

What a terrible day today. I heard the kids in the cafeteria line talking about Carrie. They said she burst into tears when she saw Danny and that Nessa rushed her to the nurse's office. Then one of them said she heard that Carrie was pregnant and probably lost the baby and that's why she went to see the nurse. Yeah, the other one said, that's probably why they broke up last month. Wow, what a mess, they said and nodded in agreement. It was all I could do not to interrupt and tell them to stop talking about Carrie when they didn't know anything about her.

I left the line and skipped lunch. I went to the library to think.

Your best friend,
Chester

I barely finished reading when I burst into tears. That's what people were doing? Talking about me? Pregnant? Lost the baby?

Oh, God. I remember that day so clearly. That truly was the beginning of the end of high school as I knew it.

It worried me that I wouldn't find out what he was hiding. But then, as I got to the end of the journal—

Journal entry: June 12, 1967

Dear Journal,

I visited my great uncle's grave tonight. That part of the cemetery is by the Old Dutch Church and very cool. I left the grave and started walking to the north side toward the Bronze Lady. I could hear voices echoing and getting louder as I got closer. What were the guys doing there tonight instead of tomorrow? Well, I figured, I'd surprise them. But the voices sounded angry so I was a bit worried to join them.

I hid behind the crypts and tall headstones as I approached. When I finally reached the Lady, it was eerily quiet except for some whimpering. I spotted Jake kneeling alone and hovering over something. It was his brother Timmy! I ran up to Jake to see if I could help but he just looked at me and told me to get the police. He looked so scared. I quickly looked down at Timmy and his head was covered with blood and he wasn't moving. I ran to the nearest house and asked them to call the police.

The police came with an ambulance but soon covered Timmy's body with a sheet. They asked me questions but I didn't tell them anything except the very end. That I found Jake kneeling over the body and Timmy not moving.

The policeman took Jake down to the police station and I guess called his parents.

It was a terrible night but I didn't tell the whole story. Maybe one day I'll even share it with you.

Your best friend,
Chester

I put down the book and, my mouth hanging open, looked straight ahead. *He was there? Is that what he meant? What's his whole story?*

I started to heave and ran to the bathroom, covering my mouth, just making it before I vomited twice. While brushing my teeth, I realized that I couldn't have stopped reading the journal even if I wanted. I headed back to the couch.

The next entry was just as bad.

June 13, 1967

Dear Journal,

I am still reeling from yesterday. I had to go to the police station and they questioned me for two hours about what I saw, what I heard, and why I went to the cemetery. My father, in the interrogation room with me, tried to explain to them that I visited the cemetery a lot and loved the solace it provided. They finally let us leave but told us I might be questioned again. I felt really scared. I'm so glad my father was with me. I might have blurted out what I really saw.

Last night, I saw them put handcuffs on Jake and put him in the police car. Jake looked out the window at me and he had tears rolling down his face. I didn't know what to do. I just waved goodbye to him.

Of course, I didn't see <u>exactly</u> what happened. But I've got a pretty good imagination.

Your best friend,
Chester

"Oh, no!" I screamed.

CHAPTER 12

THE PILLOW GAME

When Danny's parents told us they were coming up to visit for Parents Weekend in October, I feigned having a terrible flu. They told Danny they were sorry they couldn't see me but I knew they would love having Danny all to themselves.

During that weekend, I stayed in the dorm to avoid being seen by Danny's parents. I caught up on some studies in bio and history but also watched a lot of TV. One evening I joined a group of kids in the lounge watching Hawaii Five-O, a new police crime show. The episode's story centered on a man seeking revenge for his son's death. Not that I needed any reminder but my thoughts went right to Timmy. Dwelling on Timmy caused me to feel very nauseous and I ran from the room to the group bathroom.

I heard Linda, a friend on my floor, call to me through the stall door. "Hey, who's in there? Can I help you? Should I get someone?"

"No," I murmured. "It's Carrie, Linda. I must have eaten something that didn't agree with me."

"Well, I'll wait right here and help you when you're done."

I was very grateful for her help when I finished about five minutes later. I rinsed my mouth and she brought me to my room and tucked me into bed.

What would Danny and I do if we were confronted by Mr. or Mrs. Benson? Would we ever be able to return to Sleepy Hollow and keep this secret? Or would we end up in jail?

I tossed and turned all night and I could barely drag myself out of bed. But Danny was picking me up to walk to class so I forced myself to get ready.

Danny was excited that he spent time with his parents. He chatted all about their news of Tarrytown and Sleepy Hollow but I was not responding to his enthusiasm.

"Carrie," he said, "What's with you? Are you mad that you were alone all weekend?"

"No, not at all, Danny. I've been thinking a lot about Timmy and our secrets. It even made me physically sick. Linda had to help me back to my room. I'm not sure I ever want to go back to Sleepy Hollow to live."

"Yeah," he said. "I thought about that all weekend. I really love being around my parents, but..."

"Or will it look worse if we don't go back? Like we're hiding something?"

Danny reached for my hand. "I don't know what's best, Carrie. It's really too soon to make such big decisions. We have other stuff to deal with first," he said, patting my tummy.

"You're right. Let's get through our stuff one thing at a time."

"Danny, what are we going to do about Thanksgiving and Christmas?" I said one afternoon in early November while walking on campus. "I'm so worried about everyone finding out. I didn't sleep last night."

"You look beat, Carrie. Let's rest for a minute." He led me over to a bench by Hawkins Pond to sit. It was a relief to get off my feet. Already uncomfortable in my clothes, I used a rubber band wrapped around the buttons to close my almost zippered pants.

The maple trees around the pond were dropping their red and orange leaves so the grass near the pond's edge looked like a multicolored blanket. The sun shone onto the water, offering a lovely reflection of the blue sky overhead. The geese flew above the trees on their way to warmer climes and then landed on the water to rest.

"It's just so pretty here in the fall. Isn't it?" I said, squeezing Danny's hand as my leg nervously bounced up and down, up and down.

Danny nodded and put his hand on my knee to calm it. "We need to figure this out. The two of us are too good at avoiding things. Do you think you could get away with it for Thanksgiving?"

"If we don't have any hot days," I said with an uneasy chuckle. "I can probably just wear big sweatshirts, maybe yours, and sweaters. It will not be easy. My mother tends to be suspicious about everything."

"Maybe you can just carry around a pillow," Danny joked.

So, that's what I did. I carried around a pillow when I was in the house and pretended that I felt exhausted. It worked as a good excuse because I didn't even visit with Nessa. I missed her hugs but talked to her over the phone. My mother said that she would definitely need to clean that pillowcase. No one suspected anything and we went back to Plattsburgh after the weekend.

On the five-hour drive back to school, Danny and I talked about being back in Sleepy Hollow. He said he saw Chester at Clooney's.

"It was just the two of us for a while 'cause Nessa was working," Danny said. "Chester wanted to talk about Jake and Timmy, Jake and Timmy. I thought I was gonna go nuts."

"So, what did you do?" I asked.

"I just kept dodging him. He asked me when I had last seen Timmy. He asked why we decided to go there that night and not the next, like we had planned."

"Oh no," I said, putting my index finger in my mouth to bite my nail.

"Yeah. Luckily, a table of five walked in and my dad called me back to work. I was starting to sweat, Carrie."

I grabbed his hand. "How scary," I said, "I would have been freaking out too."

"Chester knew I was going to be working for a bit so luckily he left and I didn't see him again," Danny said.

We rode without speaking for a few miles. I was imagining all kinds of things and thankful I didn't see Chester when I was home. I was glad I didn't see anyone, for that matter.

"So," Danny said. "What should our plan be for Christmas? You can't get away with carrying around a pillow again."

"I was thinking," I started. "Everyone thinks I am really exhausted because of school. Maybe I could just pretend to get mono. Right? Someone in my Teaching Math class got mono."

"Hmm," said Danny.

I turned in the car seat to face him. "I could do a whole build-up. Start next week. Say I just want to sleep all the time, headachy. Then, a few days before vacation, I'll tell them I went to the infirmary and got diagnosed."

"But won't your mom want you to come home?"

"I could tell her that I would be too exhausted to make the trip home and just stay in the dorm."

"No way am I leaving you all alone up here," Danny said, shaking his head. "No way."

"What if you just go home for Christmas and come right back?"

"But what if you need something?" he said. "I'll worry if you're alone."

"I'm sure my Resident Assistant will help me out. Do you have a better idea? I don't hear you coming up with anything!"

I guess Danny knew when to be quiet. He sat up a little straighter and after a few minutes, he said, "Carrie, I know this is stressful. I'm really sorry it all falls on you. We still have time to think about it." He reached over to squeeze my hand.

"Danny, it really is stressful. I sometimes think I just might not make it. We have wreaked havoc everywhere. And to people we love. And loved."

"I know, Carrie. I sometimes try to imagine what our lives would be like if none of this happened."

"It would have been perfect," I said, as I avoided his eyes and looked out the window.

The next day, I sat down with Olivia, my RA, in her dorm room at Harrington Hall.

"I have something important to ask," I said, preparing my lie. I had confided in her about the baby at the beginning of the semester.

"OK. Does it have anything to do with the baby?" Olivia asked. "Are you two okay?"

"Yes, we're fine. But would it be possible for me to stay in the dorm over the Christmas break?"

"Why wouldn't you want to go home, Carrie?"

"My parents are leaving a few days before break to go skiing in the Alps with friends for two weeks, and then going to Paris. I would be home alone."

"We do have arrangements for students like you. Let me check with the dorm director."

By the end of the week, Olivia stopped by my room to tell me the decision.

"It will be fine for you to stay. It turns out that Harrington Hall is the dorm chosen for housing so you won't even have to move."

"Great, Olivia! Thanks so much."

Just then, the baby kicked. I couldn't wait to tell Danny about the kick, although we warned each other not to become attached if we gave the baby up for adoption. We decided to postpone the inevitable and make that final decision after the holidays.

Danny went home to Sleepy Hollow for Christmas and I stayed in the dorm again. We survived the holidays without people at home finding out about the baby. My mother called about twice a week to check in on me and sent me care packages. I have to admit I loved the packages of chocolate chip cookies and the small servings of puddings in baby food jars.

Suddenly it was second semester and I was due at the beginning of February. Danny was a scholarship student for tuition and paying his own room and board from his savings so he gave up his room in the dorm and we moved in together into a one-bedroom apartment on Broad Street. I told my parents I had moved in with Linda so they sent the monthly payments to me directly. Danny and I both kept our meal plans and ate many of our meals on campus.

Danny was able to maintain his class schedule and I attended classes as much as possible. My professors helped me out by letting me miss class occasionally if the weather became too bad for me to drive.

Both of us were stressed to a breaking point, having silly arguments and snapping at each other. We decided to give the baby up for adoption, but were truly afraid if we saw or held the baby, we would change our minds.

At the end of January, we went to a local church to talk with the priest about the adoption process. Father Newman, a tall, bearded man, didn't know us so he asked a lot of questions.

"Why have you decided to put the baby up for adoption?"

Danny looked at me and began. "We realize the baby will be much better off with a family who can support him or her. We are too young to take on the task, Father."

"Have you talked with your families about your decision? What do your parents say?"

"We are both over eighteen," Danny said. "Our parents do not know Carrie is expecting. We are living away from home and have been able to keep them from knowing."

"I see," said Father Newman. "I will talk with my connection at Catholic Charities in New York City. I think they will want to meet with you personally and discuss the process more at length. I will call you in a few days. It looks like you're getting close, Carrie."

"Yes, Father, three weeks. Dr. Hackert at the clinic says the baby and I are very healthy. Even though I'm only eighteen, I have been eating well and trying to rest."

"Do either of you smoke or drink?" Father asked.

"I do have an occasional beer, Father," Danny said and they both laughed. "But Carrie hasn't during the pregnancy."

"All right. I will call you soon. You are welcome to visit us on Sunday. The church is always open." Father Newman gave Danny a pat on the back as we left.

Driving home, Danny glanced over at me. "What did you think?"

"He made me feel comfortable. Didn't it seem easy, Danny? But it still scares me to think that we will be handing over the baby to someone we don't know."

"Well, if it's connected with the Catholic Church, it's got to be OK. Right?"

"I guess you're right. Can we stop for ice cream?"

"Sure." Danny reached over to squeeze my hand as he made a uturn to Stewart's Ice Cream on Cornelia Street. He could never refuse me.

Father Newman called us back in two days. We set up an appointment at the church office with Sister Mary Amadeus from Catholic Charities the next day.

Before we left for our consult, I couldn't help but pace in our living room, back and forth. "I am so scared, Danny," I said. "Suppose something goes wrong and they don't take the baby? Could they change their minds at the last minute? What would we do if that happened?"

Danny came over and hugged me tight. "Carrie, please calm down. I'll be right with you. I'm sure someone wants our baby as much as we want to give it a good home."

We stood like that for a few minutes until Danny said we had to leave to make the appointment on time. Our drive to the church took only a few minutes. I couldn't decide if it went fast or took forever. I felt numb.

"Good morning, Danny and Carrie," said Father Newman. "This is Sister Mary Amadeus." She looked like every nun I had met, definitely Irish with bright blue eyes and fair skin, standing about five feet tall. But she presented as all business. I felt a little intimidated, to say the least.

"Nice to meet you," she said. "Father has filled me in on your situation and I am happy to say that we already have a family interested in your baby."

Danny squeezed my hand. *So far so good.*

"However, there are some rules I need to explain to you and receive your agreement."

Danny and I both slightly nodded.

This is so serious. She's scaring me.

"The New York legislature has repeatedly revised the Domestic Relations Law since 1961 to increase protection for biological parents. I will act as the facilitator for the process. There will be a three-day waiting period after birth for parental consent to be executed. This is to protect you both. But after those three days, the decision is irrevocable."

I still can't imagine giving our baby to someone we don't know.

She paused, tilted her head to the right, then continued. "However, because we need to remember what is best for the baby, the adoption will be closed and you will not know with whom your baby will be placed. You will sever all ties."

My head turned to meet Danny's eyes, also furrowed. *Not know?*

When Sister saw my reaction, her eyes seemed to soften. "And this may be the hardest for you both. When the baby is born, he or she will be taken immediately and you will not even be told the gender. We have been told it is easier that way. Do you have any questions?"

Do we have any questions? Why do I have to give up Danny's child? Why?

"If no," Sister continued, "then here are the papers for you to sign." She slid the three forms over to us. We read through them before we signed.

We really have no choice.

"Danny and Carrie, I can imagine this will be very hard for you both," Sister Mary Amadeus said. "However, I will tell you the family to whom your baby is going has wanted a child for a very long time. Your decision will create a wonderful, God-loving family."

"Wait," said Danny. "They've been waiting a very long time? How old are these people? Can they take care of an infant?"

Sister Mary Amadeus reached out to take Danny's hand as she rose from her chair. "We have guidelines about age, health, and income. They will provide a good home."

We stood up to follow their lead. Danny hugged me and we turned to leave.

"Please give me a call when you get to the hospital," Father Newman said. "God bless and keep you safe."

The morning my contractions started looked like a beautiful and clear day: February 28, 1968, my due date. We were still in bed at 7:30 AM and my water broke. Danny called Dr. Hackert who instructed us to meet him at the hospital. Danny was running around gathering up our things and I decided to take a shower and wash my hair.

"What are you doing, Carrie? We have to go!" He hadn't even combed his hair.

"OK. OK. Give me five minutes." *I am just delaying giving up this baby.*

Fifteen minutes later, we drove to the hospital. I had to remind Danny not to speed. I was feeling pretty good, considering I was on my way to birthing a human being. But then I started talking.

"I wonder how big the baby is. I wonder if I'll find out by accident if it's a boy or girl. I wonder what it will feel like. I wonder when we'll have another baby. I wonder—" I babbled.

"Oh my God, Carrie," Danny cut in. "Remember, try not to get so connected. It will just make it harder for you."

When we arrived and settled, the doctor came in to examine me.

"I thought you said your water broke, Carrie," the doctor said. "Looks like just your mucus plug."

"Oh. So what does that mean?"

"It means you might have a longer labor. But you are three centimeters dilated and I'm on duty here at the hospital. Let's see if you can deliver this baby today."

Four hours later, I hadn't dilated any more. The doctor decided to administer Pitocin, a drug to speed up the contractions. Unfortunately, they also became more intense.

Danny was getting impatient and kept pushing the nurse for information.

Three hours later and another dose of Pitocin, the doctor told the nurse about a complication.

"The baby is breech. I can feel the toes. Take her to delivery."

"What's happening?" I asked.

"Breech means the baby turned around and is coming out feet first, instead of leading with the head," the nurse said. "The doctor can't try to turn the baby because you're almost ready to push."

The delivery room was white and very sterile. To me, everything seemed chaotic and frightening. Looking around, everyone knew what to do. But Danny left me to go to the waiting room.

A sharp contraction hit. I let out a yell, and one of the nurses grabbed my hand. "Bear down, Carrie."

"You need to push, now!" said the doctor. "Push, Carrie, push."

I could feel something ripping at the same time I felt a rushing from my body. *Oh my God that hurts!*

Sobbing, trying to catch my breath, I yelled, "Please tell me. Boy or girl?"

But the nurses stayed busy and shared nothing, as they carried the baby away in a nondescript blanket.

My baby is gone.

CHAPTER 13

THE POWER
OF SHOULD

Chester called the next day and asked me to meet him again in Patriot's Park. The knowledge that the journal lay in the drawer in my nightstand at home weighed heavily on my mind.

I should return it to Chester. I don't like that I lied to him. I know he's looking for it and he's really upset—

My thoughts were interrupted as I approached our usual meeting spot and could see Chester pacing back and forth, his arms and hands gesticulating frantically, stopping only when he saw me.

"Are you sure you didn't see the journal?" he yelled as he ran toward me.

"No," I said as my pointer finger picked at my thumb. "Let's just sit down and think about this. Did you retrace your steps?"

"Yes! It's nowhere!"

"Chester, I've never seen you this upset. Why is this journal so special?"

Chester's eyes darted to me and then quickly away. "All of my journals are special to me. All of them."

"Then why would you even carry it around? Can't you just start another one?"

As he turned to look at me again, I feared he could see my guilt in my eyes. I quickly looked away and changed the subject. No way I was going to admit I had it.

"I had it because I was re-reading it. It was my first journal."

"Let's look around some more," I said. "Maybe someone just moved it. I remember that there were a bunch of kids playing in the creek that day. Their moms were with them. Maybe we can ask them if we see them again."

"Hmm," Chester said.

Suddenly I had a thought.

"Why don't we stop in the library next door and ask if anyone turned something in? It's a long shot but, you never know."

"OK," Chester said. "Might as well."

His pale face hung down so low his chin touched his chest. His eyes were closed as we walked. *How can I help him when it's my fault? Oh, Carrie, what a mess.*

"Want to go to Clooney's for lunch after we go to the library?" I asked. "Maybe you'll have something to celebrate."

"Sure."

But I knew his heart wasn't in it. I also knew the library or I wouldn't be able to help him. Because this time, it was different. This time, I felt different. I felt shame that my friend was suffering. But it was more important that I protect myself and find out what was in the journal.

I walked up the steps to Nora's office for my appointment. This would be our third meeting and I was starting to feel comfortable with her.

She greeted me with a warm smile and firm handshake. Walking to her seat, she laughed and said, "So, I finally found out what's going on in the basement."

"Really? Do tell."

"The powers that be are creating more office space down there," Nora said. "Should be available next spring."

"They sure are doing a lot of work on this building."

Nora nodded. "Let's get started. How have you been feeling, Carrie?"

I cleared my throat. "OK, I guess, I'm getting used to being back in town. My ex-high school boyfriend showed up in town for a while. Hard to see him."

"Why hard?"

"We had a very complicated relationship," I said. "Nothing I want to go into now. Neither of us ever married or had children."

"Have you ever thought about how he feels about how things worked out?"

"No, I haven't. The good news is that he went back to California. To stay, I hope. I shouldn't even think about it."

"You shouldn't 'should' yourself," Nora said, adding air quotes. We both laughed. "When we say that word, it implies guilt or being wrong about your feelings."

"I never thought of it that way. You're right. Sometimes I think my thoughts or fears are all encompassing."

"It's important to feel fear, Carrie. We all need to protect ourselves from life-or-death experiences that may harm us."

I nodded, listing the fears in my head: *fear of people finding out my secrets, fear of heights, fear of squirrels. That's a weird one.*

We talked at length about some of them. Nora didn't feel any of them were phobias. That was a relief.

"Let's talk about possibilities for relieving your mind and body when you feel fear," Nora said. "What does your fear feel like?"

"I definitely feel a faster heartbeat. I feel like I'm sweating everywhere, around my forehead where it hits my hair. Kind of gross."

"Can you think of anything that makes you feel better?"

"I usually try to be active, like run or do something like laundry."

"The best thing is not to fight it, Carrie. Have you ever tried visualization?"

I shook my head.

"Where is a happy place for you?"

"On the river on a beautiful sunny day."

"Ok," said Nora. "Let's try it. Close your eyes and breathe in and out."

I tried.

"No, Carrie," Nora said, "breathe slower."

I took deeper and longer breaths.

"Good. Now think of floating on the river, soaking in the sunshine."

"Mmm," I hummed.

"Continue to feel your body absorb the heat and the light."

"Wonderful," I said.

"Are you still on the river?"

I nodded.

"Open your eyes. Visualization can be done anywhere. There's no reason you can't do that every day just to calm your mind and body."

"Thank you, Nora. That might work."

"Remember that your mind may wander and leave the river but you will need to practice how to get back there."

"When is the best time to practice visualization?" I asked. "When I wake up or before bed?"

"You might want to try it at a consistent time every day. But it may help you when you start to feel anxious. Just don't try it when you're driving the car!"

I chuckled. "I think I can remember that."

"Time is just about up," Nora said. "I'd like you to work on the visualization at least a few times until our next meeting."

We set my next appointment. Leaving Nora's office, I thought of all the times I use the word "should." I am going to try to avoid it and see if my expectations feel any different.

Uncle Frank's secretary called to set up another appointment to discuss the will. As I entered his office, I hoped this meeting would be less traumatic than the first. I settled into my seat as Uncle Frank started.

"Your half-sister's lawyer, Richard Caddle from Ossining, came in to discuss Stephanie's request to contest the contents of the will," he began. "As your attorney, it is my responsibility to inform you of her request."

"OK," I said, feeling a little uneasy.

"Stephanie would like half the estate, since she is William's other child."

"But she's not my mother's child and Stephanie should not have access to that piece!"

"I agree, Carolyn," Uncle Frank said. "But there are many pieces we need to discuss."

"Can she get it? Half the estate, I mean?"

Uncle Frank shook his head. "There are four main legal reasons that a will may be overturned. First, if there is a problem with the way the will is signed and witnessed. No issue with that. Done correctly."

He looked at me and I nodded.

"The second is the mental capacity of the testator at the time of signing," he continued. "The testator, in this case, would be your father. He understood his assets, who his beneficiaries were, and the effects of the will. I would attest to that."

Uncle Frank took a drink of his coffee. "Third is intentional will fraud. That would happen if your father signed a document thinking it was something other than a will. And, last, a will would be invalid if the testator was under the influence of someone else, like a caretaker."

"It doesn't sound like any of those would be valid, right?" I asked.

"Mr. Caddle agreed with me that Stephanie has no basis and cannot petition the court because she feels the will is unfair. My next question is a personal one, though. If you don't mind."

"Go ahead," I said.

"If you ever want a personal relationship with your half-sister, you might consider amending the terms so she receives more money."

"Stephanie made it quite clear that she's not interested in knowing me," I said. "I wouldn't want her to change her mind because I gave her some money. No, I'm fine being an only child. I've figured it out."

"All right, Carolyn. I will let Mr. Caddle know that the process is over," he said. "Any questions?"

I shook my head. He came around the desk to walk me to the door and hugged me before I left the office.

CHAPTER 14

TALKING 'BOUT MY GENERATION

By 1969, the Vietnam War colored and hovered over everything. A huge Air Force base in Plattsburgh bordered the edge of town. Underlying tension between the townies, the students, and the base was ever present. More fights broke out downtown where guys were drinking and smoking pot and their bravado came into question. The students were energized and organized a candle-light vigil with speakers about social injustice. I participated but with a frightened expectation that something bad might happen. I had seen rioting on TV and heard about students being beaten with police batons. Terrifying.

At one meeting, outside people were brought in to increase involvement in the peace movement. Instead of talking strategies for peace, the meeting organizers yelled, "We have to show them we mean business!" to get people riled up.

"What's the matter with you?" Danny whispered. "Your hands are clenched and you're white as a ghost."

"I'm terrified of violence, Danny. I thought this was supposed to be about peaceful protest." My legs were unsteady as I stood up.

Danny grabbed my hand to stop me, but I pushed my way out through the crowd to leave. He stayed. I cried.

After that, I continued to participate in sit-ins at the administration building and a candlelight protest march through the town. But I was careful to listen for any threat of violence.

With all that going on in our lives, we needed to have some fun. In August, Danny heard of a concert south of Albany in a farm town named Bethel Woods.

"Let's go, relax, and listen to some great music," Danny pleaded. "We can buy tickets when we get there."

My parents had given me a 1968 Toyota Corolla on the promise that I would come home to see them, which didn't happen very often. Danny and I packed it up for a quick overnight. The drive south on the Northway and New York Thruway took three and a half hours and was smooth driving until we hit the exit for Bethel Woods. Cars were parked haphazardly on the road and the grass. There were signs for the concert ahead but we had no idea how far it would be to walk. I didn't like the uncertainty. But Danny's excitement made me laugh and rubbed off on me.

When we finally reached the concert venue after about a two mile walk, we found the fencing trampled down. The ticket booth shuttered, we walked right in with hundreds of other kids.

I thought I knew who hippies were. Danny and I even fancied ourselves to be hippies because of our beliefs in social justice. Plattsburgh had varying degrees of hippies. You knew the kids who smoked grass and were always happy. You saw the kids who wore long hair and flowing dresses and no underwear. But neither of us had ever seen anything like this music festival at Yasgur's Farm. It was an unsettling feast for the senses. It had just rained and we could smell the crispness in the air along with the body odor of hundreds of kids. The grass was soggy and stuck to our legs. The sweet smell of marijuana wafted through the air in constant streams. Bumping up against people, and there were a lot of people, left sweat and dirt rubbing from them onto you. The large speakers blared with music and everyone was yelling.

Danny pulled me along and found a small patch of dirt to put down our blanket and sit. I started breathing more normally but sitting down was very uncomfortable. People were moving in waves and it I felt dizzy constantly looking up to see them. I made myself look at Danny or anything else at eye level.

"Isn't this great?" Danny said, pulling me back to reality. "Holy shit. Just look at this, Carrie. Look where we are. This is a happening."

"It is something," I said as I grabbed the beer he offered. I had to admit that the music sounded really good, when I could hear it. So much noise.

The next band to play was the Grateful Dead. Finally, someone I recognized. Their last song had long been a favorite of mine, "Let Your Love Shine on Me." Danny turned and sang the lyrics to me.

I was okay, sitting in one place with Danny. We were talking with other kids around us who had come from all over the state. After a few beers, I started to relax. But it was another story when we left our blanket to find a bathroom.

"The bathrooms are out of order," a policeman told us.

"Well, guess it's the woods!" Danny said, almost cheerfully.

I glared at him. Going in the woods was a hell of a lot easier for him. Needless to say, there was no privacy and I was horrified. I felt exposed to men who didn't know or love me. I felt their eyes on me, sure I was being judged. Like Timmy.

The worst happened as I was coming out of the woods, trying to find Danny. A guy stumbled toward me and knocked me down. He was dirty, his hair was long and sweaty, and his eyebrows furrowed with fear as he started yelling at me.

"Why are you following me everywhere?" he said. "I'm not the one you should be looking for. Stay away!"

He pushed Danny as he approached and ran away, careening into anyone else in his path.

"Whoa, that guy's on a bad trip," Danny said. "Hope he doesn't hurt himself or anyone else."

Making our way back to the blanket, there seemed to be a pause in the noise and I heard a piercing scream. I looked around. There was a young woman about four rows behind us with a tiny baby, crying very loudly.

"Oh my God, Danny. Someone brought a baby to this hell hole!"

He grabbed for me as I pushed my way to the baby.

"Carrie, stop!"

By the time I reached them sitting on a tattered blanket, the mother had pulled out her breast and tried to nurse. The baby fussed for a moment more before finally latching on. The woman glanced at me and smiled but I could not look away from that intimate moment. I never had that moment. I wonder if my baby could feel that I wasn't the one who fed her.

Isn't the noise going to hurt the baby's ears? I continued to look at the now contented and quiet baby. *She should cover that baby's ears.*

I was angry at this woman and was about to admonish her when someone turned me around and hugged me tight.

"Carrie, stop. I know you're upset but that's not our baby nor is it our place to say anything," Danny whispered in my ear.

I pulled away and he wiped away my tears.

"I know, Carrie. I know. Let's go back and sit down."

We returned to our blanket and someone passed us a joint. I grabbed for it, inhaled, and coughed loudly. I took another toke and my body finally felt calm.

The Who started playing at about 5 AM. A rally cry went through the entire crowd when they played their final song in a really long set. The frenzied crowd jumped up and down and sang as one about "my generation." Still feeling a bit high, the lyrics resonated with me, especially the last line about dying before we got old.

We left after that. I was not doing the bathroom in the woods again. Getting out of there was a nightmare, stepping over tangles of bodies. People were shedding clothes and dancing with uninhibited madness. I was glad we were leaving; it was over the top for me at that point.

The muddy road back to the car turned out to be like navigating a maze, all different makes of cars left at crazy angles, seemingly just abandoned. We finally found our car and it took Danny about another hour just to drive us out of there. We stopped at the first gas station we passed to use the rest room.

There are many important dates I carry in my heart. The JFK assassination on November 22, 1963. Martin Luther King's assassination on April 4, 1968, followed by Bobby's murder on June 6, 1968. It was a tumultuous time to be alive.

Other than my child's birth date, December 1, 1969 is another date I will never forget.

Ten of us sat in our living room around the TV that night, a solemn tenseness in the air.

"*Mayberry RFD* will not be presented tonight. It will return next week on this station. The Draft Lottery. A live report on tonight's picking of the birthdays for the draft. Here is Roger Mudd…"

We had no idea what to expect, only a hope that our guys would be spared. I sat next to Danny, our hands entwined as he kept trying to loosen my grip. He let go as he grabbed the bottle of cheap wine that was being shared to take a huge gulp.

"It'll be fine, Carrie. Don't worry."

We listened in horror as September 14 became the first date chosen. Danny's birthday. Danny was drafted. He was going to war.

And I would be alone.

There was a sense of chaos in the room. Some of our friends were screaming and grabbing for Danny.

"Oh my God, Danny!" said Lynn.

"You need to go to Canada tomorrow!" said Roger.

"Everyone, shut up!" said another. "We need to hear the next dates."

Suddenly, I couldn't hear or even see anything. Everything seemed to come to a stop in the room. Danny reached for me as I started to feel faint and my legs wobbled as we headed for the bedroom.

"Can't you get a deferment, Danny?" I asked. "You're in school full-time."

"I need to serve, Carrie. What would happen if everyone deferred?"

"I don't care about everybody. I care about you. And me."

I guess our friends watched the screen for the next dates to be called. No one else turned out to be as unlucky as Danny that night. The other boys had high numbers or were not called at all. The high numbers would probably be able to finish college. Anyone with a low number had to go, unless someone was exempt because of illness or had children.

I mumbled to Danny, "If you had a child, you wouldn't have to go, Danny."

"Shhhh," Danny said, stroking my hair.

We clung to each other and cried.

The phone calls started from the family. I could only hear Danny's responses.

"I need to finish the semester, Ma," Danny said. "I also don't know when I will have to report. But I'll definitely come home to see you before I leave for boot camp."

Boot camp. They made it sound like fun.

"I'll be fine, Ma. Can I talk to Pops?" Danny grimaced as he looked at me.

"Hi, Pops. Yeah, who can believe it?"

Pause.

"No deferment for me. I need to serve. You served. So did Grandpop."

Pause.

"I have no idea where boot camp will be. Guess I'll see a different part of the country."

Pause.

"No, none of my buddies got low numbers. Luck of the Irish, I guess."

Pause.

"Yeah, bye. Love you guys. Talk to you soon," Danny said.

When we came out into the living room, everyone had gone and the television was turned off. We headed back to the bedroom to try to sleep. I worried our lives would never be the same. But Danny promised he would come back to me.

When Danny left for the war, I retreated to my apartment like a hermit. I didn't look for another roommate. Our friends eventually stopped calling but Danny's letters in the beginning were filled with expressions of love for me and hopes that we would resume our lives when he came home. We wrote of marriage and family, although there were no decisions made about returning to our hometown. Then the letters dwindled from once a week to twice a month. After eighteen months, Danny's letters were filled with anger about the war and Viet Nam and little about us. Then, the letters stopped after about two years. I felt distraught and helpless. I continued to write to him for another year but didn't hear back. The lack of communication confused me and I worried about his safety. I called Nessa to check with his parents but he had even stopped writing to them.

I had lost some class time after the baby so I didn't graduate until December of 1972. I blamed it on the mono. I told my parents not to bother coming to the ceremony because I didn't want to go. They put up a little fight and I finally agreed. The graduation was uneventful as I knew no one else who graduated.

I traveled home to Sleepy Hollow to catch up with my parents and Nessa.

"We are very proud of you, Carolyn," Father said at dinner that evening.

Mother added, "You have had a lot to overcome. Yes, we are proud of you."

"What are your plans?" Father asked.

"I'm going to substitute teach this semester and hopefully find a job for the fall," I said. *I know what's coming.*

"Where are you going to look for a job?" Mother said. "We are hoping you would come back to Sleepy Hollow."

There it was.

"Matter of fact," said Father. "Your mother and I would like to give you $10,000 for a down payment on a house to start you off. In Sleepy Hollow, as your mother said."

My mouth dropped open, my chin dipped, and my eyes grew large. "That's amazing," I said.

My parents looked at each other and smiled.

"So glad, Carolyn," Mother said. "We've missed you."

"Oh, but I think I'm going to stay in Plattsburgh to work. I can still have the money, right?"

Their smiles turned to frowns and their eyebrows furrowed. I could tell they didn't expect that.

"Well, ah, I don't know," Father said.

"But it's my graduation present," I said. "I should be able to use it however I want. A house would be an incredible investment. I wouldn't need much."

"We won't be able to help you find a house there, Carolyn," Mother said.

"I'm a big girl. I'll call to ask questions and find a good realtor. I'll even let you choose the company."

"All right. But if it doesn't work out and you want to come home to look, let us know," Father said. "We will help you out."

I'm free! And, when Danny comes home, that can be our starter house.

I couldn't wait to see Nessa and give her a big hug. Of course, we dined at Clooney's. Mr. Clooney congratulated me for graduating and I told him I would be substitute teaching in Plattsburgh. I hoped I would find a job before summer for next September.

"Mr. Clooney, do you hear from Danny?" I asked.

"Not too often. Last we heard he was still in Nam but thought he might be getting out soon."

"Glad to hear he's OK," I said. We exchanged a sad smile. Mr. Clooney wiped his clean bar again and threw the towel over his shoulder.

"Dinner's on me, Carrie. Happy graduation!"

Such a nice man. I miss them as much as I miss Danny.

Nessa had graduated from the police academy and now worked as a beat cop in Tarrytown. The force was happy to have her working there. The only female in the department, they called on her often, especially when dealing with domestic situations.

"The department is treating me well but there are still guys who struggle 'cause I'm a woman," she said, peeling off the label on the bottle of beer. "I think they feel they can't trust my instincts."

"But they have so much respect for your father," I said. "I would think they'd be nicer to you."

"They have respect for him 'cause he's earned it. I have a ways to go."

"What exactly do you do as a beat cop?"

"I actually really like it," said Nessa. "A beat is a territory and time that a police officer patrols. It uses the close relationship with the community within that beat to strengthen our effectiveness. We want people to cooperate with us to make Tarrytown safer."

"I can see why you like it. You love this community."

"Yes, I do. Toast," as she lifted her beer. "To us as we start our lives as grownups."

"Cheers," I said, clinking her bottle. But my future still felt uncertain.

PART TWO

CHAPTER 15

FEAR OF SQUIRRELS

Nessa's interview in Poughkeepsie in October broke open the case of the raped young woman and the burning car at the train station. Nessa's contact had connected two men with the attack on the woman now identified as Patricia Fuller. Nessa shared the details of the investigation during our hike around the Tarrytown Lakes in March. We sat on the grass overlooking the section of the water where we skated in high school during the winter.

"Patricia was the common-law wife of one of the men accused," Nessa said. "She threatened to leave and turn him in for selling drugs. He raped her and then had one of his friends bring some gas to light up the car. Poor woman. She never had a chance."

"What a sad story, Nessa. You must feel great about getting her justice. Good job."

"They've been charged with murder and sexual assault." She paused. "We did get the bad guys. But it doesn't bring her back or help her family. Heinous way to die. They better throw the book at them."

"When is the trial?" I asked.

"Should be in about six months. But you never know with lawyers."

Nessa muttered some curse words under her breath, dismissing the thought with a wave of her hand and lighting up her third cigarette in less than an hour. I knew better than to ask her to translate.

Two nights later on a cold and rainy evening, I waited for Nessa at Clooney's. I couldn't help but think about Chester. He was still reticent around me and wouldn't look me in the eyes. I thought if I got him alone, I might bring up the night Timmy died and, without mentioning the journal entry, get him to talk about what he remembered. Just then, Nessa burst through the door, drenched and cursing.

I burst out laughing. "Wow, Nessa. What a mess!"

"I freaking hate thunderstorms. I hate being so wet. Pisses me off."

Mr. Clooney came over and told Nessa, "One Hot Toddy coming up for you, Nessa. How about you, Carrie?"

I nodded. Nothing wrong with warming your insides.

We were deep in conversation, drinking our hot toddies when the door flew open and a young man came in, his face covered by a rain hat, shaking his umbrella before placing it by the door.

"Hello, Keith," said Mr. Clooney. "Thanks for coming out on such a terrible night."

"Sure thing," he said. He sat in the booth behind us with his back to us and the door. Mr. Clooney took his order and he opened a newspaper.

"Well, hello," Mr. Clooney said, as Chester walked through the door. "How about a hot toddy for you?"

"Sure, thanks," Chester said as he sat down next to me.

Hmm. Now he doesn't have to look at me.

And that is exactly what happened. He directed all of his eye contact and talk to Nessa. But I don't think she realized I was being snubbed.

"I was afraid of thunderstorms when I was little," Chester said, surprising me and Nessa. I thought it unusual for him to admit something about himself.

"What are you afraid of, Nessa?" I asked.

"Not too much, really. Of course, I'm afraid of being shot but I can't think about that too much. For obvious reasons. How about you, Carrie?"

I'd be afraid of being shot too. That's not surprising.

"Oh, the list is too long. But I'll settle for squirrels."

"What?" Nessa laughed. "Mija, they are so cute."

"They are just furry rats," I said, shuddering. "Ew. They can bite you and carry diseases."

"Fear of squirrels is calls Sciurophobia," said Chester. Nessa and I both sat up straighter and turned to look at him with our mouths open.

"The best fear I learned about at the museum is hippopotomonstroses. Know what that is?" said Chester, clearly in his element.

We both shook our heads. "It's the fear of long words!" he said. "Isn't that great?"

We heard the guy in the next booth chuckle. I guess it was hard not to hear us.

"I am just amazed you know that, Chester," Nessa said. I lifted my drink and we toasted him. He beamed and I could tell he felt proud that he impressed us. But he never looked at me.

I would have to wait to talk with Chester when I had him alone.

CHAPTER 16

A FACE IN THE WINDOW

The first morning in April, I found a large manila envelope on my doorstep when I got back from my run. I saw the return address, then grabbed onto the railing to keep from falling. It read Sing Sing Prison, Ossining, New York. Jake. I hadn't heard a thing from him in fifteen, no twenty years. I turned the envelope over. No postmark.

No way I can open that right now. How the hell could Jake send me a letter?

I shoved the envelope under the pile of mail. The dishes in the sink became a surprising priority. I emptied and refilled the dishwasher and waited for the package to explode or something. Then I heard the beep from the dryer and started to fold and hang up laundry. But I knew it was there. The envelope. I needed to work up courage to open it. My chest felt like it seized up. I started to dry heave before I even got to the bathroom.

How am I going to face this? This can't be good news, right?

I picked up the envelope from the desk and walked out to the sunroom.

The return address was confusing and alarming. Jake had committed suicide in prison in 1970. He hung himself with bedsheets. Another thing Danny and I had never discussed. I wrote him in Vietnam but he never responded to my letter.

I went to the dining room and found a bottle of Scotch whiskey in the bar. My father always kept it stocked with the "best liquor money can buy," he used to say. I didn't care that it was 9:30 in the morning. I needed it.

After pouring myself a shot, I looked long and hard at that sweet liquid in the glass. I closed my eyes, put the glass to my nose and took a strong whiff. Then I savored the taste. The burning in my chest gave me courage. I ripped open the package. Inside were two envelopes. The crinkled, tattered one was addressed to my maiden name with my parents' address from twenty years ago that had been returned to sender. They must not have accepted it because it came from the prison. It looked nasty and smelled like smoke.

One more drink to get through this.

I poured another drink and opened the letter. Jake proclaimed his appreciation to me for visiting him in jail and writing to him. He apologized for kissing me when I was so vulnerable. I could almost see his face. And then I needed another swig to clear my head of those cobwebs.

Barely able to stop my hands from trembling, I opened the second envelope addressed only with my first name. This one appeared newer and cleaner than the first. He said he had missed me over the years. The letter ended by saying he hoped we would be reunited soon.

As I sat back to finish the last of my drink and think about the letters, I glanced up.

And choked. And spit out my drink all over the papers and table.

An image in the window. A face. Jake's face!

I screamed and stood up, knocking the table and spilling the drink all over me. As I looked back toward the window, the image was gone. I ran and peered out but saw no one except the landscape guys.

Did I just imagine that? Was it the liquor? Am I hallucinating?

I bolted out the door and waved my hands at the landscaper on the riding mower until he saw me and stopped. I must have looked a little out of my mind. I didn't care.

"Sorry to stop you. Did you see anybody out here near the window? A young guy with dark hair? Just a few minutes ago?"

"Yeah, I did. I figured he was a friend of yours or someone doing an estimate for something. Why? You need help?"

"No. You saw him. That's good. That's good," I said as I turned to walk back into the house.

He saw him. I saw him.

I ran around checking the locks on all the doors. Then I called Nessa and curled into a fetal position on the couch.

But Jake is dead.

Nessa came by an hour later during her lunch break. She sat down at the table and took out her sandwich. "What's up?"

"You went to Jake's funeral, right? Jake killed himself in jail. Right?"

"Whoa, Mija. You know I did. What's this about?"

I dropped the envelopes on the table. "I got these this morning." I worked on a hangnail that was begging to be pulled with my teeth.

Nessa picked them up off the table. "Good news does not come in envelopes that smell like that. It's from Sing Sing?"

"So it says. How is that possible?"

"Looks like it was mailed a long time ago."

"I'm pretty sure my parents didn't accept delivery because it came from Sing Sing. I actually had to have a drink before I could read it."

I grabbed a tissue from the counter and dabbed my hangnail, now bleeding. I always like that feeling of ripping it off and making it bleed. Kind of satisfaction for a job well done. I glanced up again at Nessa. Did I see a crinkling around her eyes?

"Would you read them so you'll know why I'm so freaked out?" I asked.

"Sure." Nessa opened the envelopes and scanned the letters. Creases of anger in her forehead worsened the more she read. Nessa jumped up out of her chair, glaring at me. "Who sent these to you?"

That second drink didn't touch the panic attack I felt coming.

"Are these from Jake? What does it mean he was apologizing for kissing you? He was my boyfriend, Carrie! I don't understand."

Nessa's brow was furrowed and she looked directly into my eyes.

"OK. Full disclosure. I am so sorry, Nessa. It was only once. Danny and I had broken up and I was having a terrible time and..."

"And so you helped yourself to someone else's boyfriend. I knew you had secrets," she said as she stormed out, slamming the door.

After Nessa ran out of my house, I must have called her twenty times with no success. But I had to make this right and dialed again.

"Hello," she said.

"Please don't hang up, Nessa. It's me."

"What can you possibly say to me, Carrie?"

"Nessa, Jake and I never did anything except kiss one time. It didn't mean anything. I just needed someone to comfort me. That was all."

Nessa paused. "I wasn't good enough?" I heard the sadness in her voice.

"We can't do this over the phone," I said. "Can we talk in person? Please meet me at Clooney's. Would 3:00 work?"

"I'll see if I can get there. Bye." The click from her hanging up stung in my ear.

What would I do if Nessa didn't forgive me? Chester was still wary of me. I wouldn't have a friend any more if I didn't have her.

Three o'clock couldn't come soon enough for me. I did some busy work around the house, laundry and kitchen clean-up. I wanted to see and talk with Nessa. When I arrived at Clooney's, I sat facing the door, trying to look relaxed. Mr. Clooney appeared and I ordered a scotch on the rocks. He guffawed as he watched me twist and rip up a napkin.

"You're a wee bit nervous today, Carrie," he said. "Meeting anyone?"

"Yes, sir," I said. "Nessa should be here soon."

At 4:30, still alone, I decided to give up. I waved goodbye to Mr. Clooney and bumped into Nessa at the door.

"Oh, sorry," she said, avoiding my eyes. "I got stuck at work."

I didn't complain. At least she had come. We slid into a booth as Mr. Clooney took our orders. Another drink for me and Budweiser for Nessa. She was off-duty.

I knew I had to start the conversation but I felt a bit intimidated. She had her serious cop-face on with her eyes boring into me, her shoulders hunched toward me as she leaned in with her arms crossed on the table. I leaned back to be a little farther from her face and bumped my head on the wooden booth.

"Ow!" I said. "Well, I guess that served me right." We both chuckled. I saw my "in."

"Nessa, I hope you know that I am really sorry but...no, I'm not going to say any buts. No excuses for me. Just reasons."

"I'm listening," Nessa said, tapping her fingers on the table.

"You know all that I was going through back then?" She nodded. "Well, I never told you all of it. Believe me there was a lot more. Maybe someday I'll tell you everything. But not yet. I'm not ready. Even after all this time."

Nessa took a swig of her beer.

I started to explain. "What I will tell you is I remember waiting for you to join us after Danny broke up with me and I was blathering on Jake's shoulder and it…just…happened. We only kissed once. I had been drinking so I thought it was Danny. Weird, I know. Jake said we had to stop because it wasn't fair to you."

"I did feel like I deserted him when he was convicted," said Nessa. "But my father told me to keep my distance so I didn't even write to him." She let out a deep sigh. "I really cared for him."

"I know you did. And he cared for you. I was as surprised as you when I got that letter. Maybe it was because I called him in prison before I went to school? I know you couldn't because you were applying to the academy. Chester did, which I never quite understood. It was nice of him but kind of weird. Jake sure needed friends. Poor Jake."

"Carrie, the kiss isn't really what bothered me. It's the secrets. It's very frustrating and hurtful for me as your longtime friend."

I reached out for Nessa's hand. She grabbed it back and squeezed. I immediately burst into tears and Nessa called out, "Another Bud for me, Mr. Clooney."

"I didn't even get to tell you about the face in the window," I said to Nessa. "I swear to God I saw Jake."

"Mija, you know that's not possible."

"But someone was there because I ran out and asked the landscaper. He saw somebody. I didn't imagine it."

"It's obvious this 'somebody' resembled Jake," Nessa said. "Did he have any cousins? But why would they bother you?"

No, I don't know about any cousins—

"And Jake and Timmy both died before they had any kids," she continued.

*That we know of…*and then an awful thought hit me. *Oh my God—*

"Mija, you OK? You look white as a ghost."

"I think I might get sick," I said, putting my head down on the table.

He looked like Jake.

Nessa bolted to the bar to get a cold cloth and some ice cubes.

I lifted my head and stared straight at nothing, tuning Nessa out.

But I was never with Jake. Oh, no. Please.

"Carrie, let me help you. Here," she put the cloth on the back of my neck and on my forehead. "I'm taking you home."

It can't be. He looked like Timmy!

She led me out the door and into her car. As I sat in the passenger seat, my body started to tremble.

Could it be that my baby was Timmy's?

The possibility that my baby had been Timmy's preoccupied my thoughts. *Since Danny left, maybe I wouldn't have to tell him. We thought the baby was created with love, not from some monster. How would I react if I ever met him or her?*

That weekend, Nessa asked me to go to a Phish concert at the Capitol Theater in Port Chester, about twenty minutes away. I knew nothing about the band, but Nessa filled me in on our drive.

"Great alternative music with talented musicians," she said. "Phish started in Vermont a few years ago. People say they sound like the Grateful Dead but I like Phish better."

Nessa exposed me to a lot of different music so I knew it would be a fun night.

After parking, we found a seat to the right side of the stage.

"What do you think of this place?" said Nessa. "It was renovated in the late '60s to be a psychedelic performance hall. Crazy, right?"

I looked around. "But has some of it been renovated again?"

"Yeah, good eye," Nessa said. "It was closed during the '70s and '80s because of the economy so they're trying to start again."

"It's a great venue for a band," I said. "Can't wait!"

I was impressed that Phish didn't have an opening band. Nor did they stop for an intermission. But about an hour into the concert, I looked to my left when people started standing to clap their hands or dance. That's when I spotted her—Stephanie Conway.

My half-sister didn't see me. She was laughing and throwing her hands up in the air. As surprised as I was, it was nice to see her having so much fun. I leaned to my left to whisper to Nessa to look, when I stopped and sharply inhaled.

Standing with her to her left, a man met my gaze. I noticed that my neck stiffened and then tingled.

I've seen him before. Why is my neck tingling?

He raised his chin in recognition. He never broke eye contact.

He was the man in my window!

I could feel the control with his uneven, insolent smile.

He's smirking at me.

"Oh my God," I said to Nessa. "It's him."

"What? Who?"

In the moment that I looked at Nessa, he was gone. I stood up and frantically looked around, but didn't see him. I saw Stephanie though.

Did he follow me here? Was that Timmy's son?

Nessa was rocking out to the music and never heard what I said. I left to go to the restroom. *How did he know my half-sister?*

He wasn't in the lobby. I waited to see if he came out of the restroom. When he didn't, I went back to my seat and after the encore, we left the venue.

Driving home, Nessa couldn't stop talking about Trey this, Trey that. I remembered that Trey was one of the band members but I was consumed.

Who was that man? Am I imagining all of this?

"Nessa, I need to tell you something."

"Oh, what?"

"I saw the guy from my window at the concert."

"Really?" Nessa said. She glanced at me, her eyebrows furrowed.

"I know you must think I've lost it. But it was him. He looked right back at me."

"Aye, Mija."

"And here's the worst part. He was with Stephanie! My half-sister!"

"You must be mistaken. How would he know her?"

I thought for a moment. "Maybe they weren't together because he left without her after I saw him. But he stood next to her and watched me."

"Mija, maybe you need to tell the police." Nessa turned to me. "Well, I mean go to the police station and put in an official report that someone is bothering you."

"I'll think about it. Hopefully, he will just leave me alone."

"I mean it, Mija," Nessa said, pointing her index finger at me. "If it happens again, we're going."

CHAPTER 17

THE TIP OF THE ICEBERG

My next session with Nora had signs of a breakthrough for me, although I was determined to hold back from her. We were talking about my parents and their concerns about looking perfect to everyone.

"I would get so sick of them talking to me about nothing," I said. "Nothing that was important."

"Important to whom? You?"

"Yes," I said.

"Maybe it was important to them, Carrie."

"Ugh."

"It sounds to me like they had a very different way of communicating," Nora said, as she checked her notes. "They were married for a long time, right?"

"Yes, forty-six years. But it seemed to me that they never spoke about feelings or nice things about other people. It reminded me of that picture of the iceberg. Have you seen that?"

"No, I don't think so."

"The poster hung in my fifth-grade classroom. The kids loved it. It showed how much of the iceberg people see from above the water. But most of the iceberg, the important part, is underneath and hidden."

"What does that mean to you?"

"I only saw the tip of the iceberg with my parents. Never saw under the water, so to speak."

"That's a great metaphor, Carrie. Am I just seeing the tip of the iceberg in our sessions?" Nora's sober look told me she was earnest.

I nodded my head, looking away. When I turned back, I found her eyes and said, "That was a fair question. I'll work on it."

"Returning to your parents," Nora said, "Can you think of any reason why they 'talked about nothing' in front of you?"

I chuckled. She had used air quotes.

"Maybe they thought I wouldn't understand. Maybe they thought I would reject them."

"That's interesting, Carrie. Would you have rejected them?"

"Maybe," I said. "I did discover something interesting about my mother. She hired a PI."

"A private investigator?"

"Yes, and I called and spoke with him," I said. "She knew about Stephanie. The PI reported to her every two months for fifteen years."

"Wow," Nora said. "Going back to your concerns that they talked about nothing in front of you, how did this discovery make you feel?"

"Again," I said. "This would have been relevant to me and they said nothing."

Nora looked at me. "Did you ever try to talk about something that was of importance to you?"

"No. It would have been too much effort on my part," I said.

"Has this ever happened in any other relationship? How about with Nessa?"

"Well, yes. She got very mad at me about something that happened in our past but she didn't seem to care how I felt when it happened. Actually, it was our first argument."

"Carrie, did you tell her how you felt?"

I shook my head.

"Did you try to imagine how Nessa felt?"

"Actually, no," I said. "I was just concerned about me." My eyes started to well up.

I had been a terrible friend to Nessa. Did our friendship revolve around me and my issues?

"Carrie," Nora said. "Are you practicing visualization?"

"Yes," I said. "But I don't think I'm doing it correctly. It sometimes brings up some bad memories or weird thoughts."

"That's not unusual when you're first starting the practice. Would you like to try it now so I can talk you through it?"

"Yes," I said, settling back in my chair.

"Good," Nora said. "I see you're getting comfortable. Now, let's go to your peaceful place—the boat on the river on a beautiful sunny day. You can feel the warmth of the sun on your face and your body is relaxed."

"Mmm," I murmured.

"How are you feeling, Carrie?"

"Oh, oh! There's a big black crow covering the sun. Go away, go away!" I felt my arms swinging in front of me as it fell from the sky.

"I want you to stop now, Carrie," Nora said. "Can you feel your feet on the ground? Put your hands in your lap."

I did as she instructed. The image of the bird went away.

Nora continued. "Can you tell me what that was like, Carrie?"

"I felt my arms swinging," I said. "I guess I was afraid the bird was going to attack me."

"What did you notice in your mind?" she said. "Do you know where the black bird came from?"

"No, no," I said tentatively.

Oh. I read that Chester had a black bird in his dream. I wonder if I was thinking about that.

"It could be just a figure to block out the sun," Nora said. "A dying bird in dream interpretation can mean unending worries."

"Well, that's appropriate," I said.

"I would keep trying to practice, Carrie," Nora suggested. "If your troubling thoughts start to take over, remember that you can ground yourself and take back control."

"All right. Maybe we can practice a few more times when I come back."

"Sure," Nora said. "How is everything else?"

"I feel like damaged goods, Nora," I said. "I feel broken from my secrets. I keep people at arm's length."

"I won't tell you that what you're feeling is wrong, Carrie," Nora said. "But I will tell you that, although you have had trauma in your life, things are not irreparable. You are doing the right thing by trying to work through them. I'm here when you want to talk about them."

The next day on my run, I tried desperately not to think about the concert. I looked at the houses I passed and realized that I hadn't noticed details about them, like the beautiful landscaping resplendent with mature trees and colorful bushes. I approached my house, making a mental note to call the landscaper to put in more flowers, something to bring in an abundance of color. Maybe that would distract me.

Back home, I decided to clean out the guest room and found more designer dresses and even a tux in the closet. The consignment store where I brought the Chanel suit hadn't called back about the that piece, but I thought the owner might be interested in these also. If she didn't want the tux, maybe she could give me other options.

Clearing the closet moved quickly because I either threw everything into the trash or into a donation box. I had to get the small ladder my father kept in the garage to reach the top shelves.

Tucked away on the very top one, my hand found one of those old cigar boxes. A variation of yellows with the brand name King Edward the Seventh, Mild Tobaccos emblazoned on the top of the box brought back memories of my father when he gave me a box like this for my childhood treasures.

I used to have one just like this but I threw it out a long time ago.

Red stickers repeating the name bordered the top with a white drawing on the middle of each side of two horses and a crown. A trademark created with two cursive capital letters S completed the picture.

I gasped as I opened the top. It was my box of special things. *How did this get here?*

My mother must have taken it out of the garbage that day we argued so long ago. I remembered that argument clearly. It was the day Danny broke up with me, back in 1967. I entered the kitchen, headed for the trash can.

"What are you doing, Carolyn?" Mother had said, turning from the sink.

"I'm throwing this out. I don't want anything to remind me of this family."

"Why in heaven's name would you say that?" she asked.

"You and Father have never cared about what I want. I know you are glad Danny broke up with me. His father's a bar owner. That's not good enough for you!"

I dumped the box into the trash.

"Carolyn, wait!"

"No!" Slamming the door, I went for a run and assumed the box was gone forever. Mother never said anything about it when I returned from my run.

Now, here I was twenty years later, holding that box. Why did my mother fish it out of the trash? Why didn't she ever tell me she kept it? Did she keep it for me, or for her?

I stepped off the ladder and sat on the bed with the box. As I opened it, I leaned it to take a small whiff and remembered the cigars wrapped in cellophane with that same red label on the top of the box. My father loved his cigars, although Mother made him go outside to smoke. I disliked the smell of the smoke but was fascinated by the ritual of cutting the cigar with the special tool, lighting it, and then sitting back to relax.

I never realized how beautiful the boxes were, even on the inside lid. There was a picture of King Edward, with his reddish hair and bushy mustache and beard, looking very regal. Meant to be part of the advertisement on a shelf, a small circle on the outside announced that each cigar cost seven cents.

Wow. This takes me back.

I started to take out each of my memories one by one. Three ice-skating medals I won when I was thirteen: one gold, two bronze. Seashells from Jones Beach. Tickets from SHHS football games. A patch from the back of my jeans that Danny had ripped off with his teeth on a dare from Jake. The ticket from the train Danny, Nessa, Jake, and I took on New Year's Eve to travel into the city to watch the ball drop. A Christmas card from Chester. Silly things.

Mother must have added the next items because I had not. An old piece of waxed paper caught my eye. Inside was a rose that had been pressed between book pages for a long time. Written on the paper in faded ink, I read "Carolyn's gift from her father" and my birthdate. Next came programs from my graduations from Sleepy Hollow High School and Plattsburgh State University. I found all of this surprising. Mother didn't seem the sentimental type.

Hidden underneath the school programs were prayer cards from Transfiguration Church from Timmy's and Jake's funerals. Inside Jake's card was his death notice from the newspaper, dated October 2, 1971.

But at the very bottom was a picture turned over with the words on the back, "Carolyn, Plattsburgh, January 1968."

What is this?

I felt my heart skip a beat. It was a picture of me with my pregnant belly in Plattsburgh!

Oh, Mother. You knew and never said anything to me? Where did this come from?

I had a fitful sleep that night but awoke with thoughts about the picture of me and my pregnant belly in Plattsburgh.

Vernon Jones, my mother's PI, had sent me the written reports of my father's surveillance. I wanted to call and thank him but also to ask something else.

"Hi Carrie," Vernon said. "Did you get the reports? Any questions?"

"Yes, I did. Thanks. No questions about *them*," I said, emphasizing the last word.

"Oh? You have other questions?"

"Yes." I paused. "Vernon, did my mother ask you to spy on me my freshman year in college at Plattsburgh?"

"Well," he laughed. "I wouldn't call it spying."

"Whatever you did. Did you take a picture of me in the winter of 1968?"

"Yes, I did. Don't feel scared though. I didn't hang around and watch you. Just waited near Hawkins Hall on campus and took a few photos of you."

"That's so creepy," I said, shivering.

"Your mother suspected something was going on. Did she ever talk with you about your pregnancy?"

"No, and I never told her."

"Sorry about that, Carrie," Vernon said. "I liked your mother. She seemed to be dealing with a lot."

We all were.

"At least now I know who took the picture. Thanks, Vernon."

"Take care and let me know if you need anything else."

"OK. Bye." We hung up.

CHAPTER 18

RAMPING UP

Nessa and I were in Clooney's when I realized that Danny had returned to Sleepy Hollow.

"Aye, ladies," Mr. Clooney said to us. "Our Danny is home to stay!"

"It's easy to see how happy you are, Mr. C," Nessa said, as I gulped down my drink.

My anxiety really ramped up knowing that Danny came home. And on top of seeing the face in the window, Chester was still not talking to me. On more than one night I drowned my sorrows at Clooney's and had stumbled home, mumbling disjointed thoughts about my past.

Nessa brought me home that night; she had to leverage her weight against mine at the doorway to keep me up. She pushed me up the stairs to the bedroom and plopped me onto the bed.

Her faraway voice told me that I resembled some of the drunks she arrested.

"I wish I knew what the hell you were saying, Carrie. What does, 'he's evil, he's evil' mean? I'm getting tired of seeing you like this every night. We're going to talk about this soon."

"Nessa, I really love you. But you don't know, you…"

"We're also going to have to buy you a different cologne. I cannot believe you have worn Jean Nate every day since high school. Yuk. Tired of it."

That was the last thing I heard. I guess I passed out. Nessa must have set the alarm for the next morning before she left to drive home because it went off in the morning, just in time for my run.

When I returned from my run that next morning, I found Nessa sitting on my front steps.

"How about some coffee and talk?" she said.

"I'm so embarrassed," I said, after sitting down with our coffee. "Sorry you had to take care of me." I hid my fake smile behind my hand.

"OK, Carrie," Nessa said. "Something is going on. You went from casual drinking to excessive drinking, like overnight."

"I know."

"I haven't seen you drink like that since Prom night," Nessa said. "Of course, you've been away for a long time but you didn't even drink when you came home. Don't you think you can talk to me?"

"I, um, guess I've been keeping things down for a long time."

"Honestly? I don't think you're playing fair. Keeping secrets."

My mouth dropped open. "Why do you think that?"

"First, that thing with Jake that I found out only because you were freaked out by the face in the window. And now you think that guy is stalking you."

"Well," I started.

"And I totally don't understand why Chester is not talking to you," Nessa said. "This whole thing is just bizarre, Carrie. Too much is happening to not have secrets that you are hiding."

I sat with my head hung down. *God, I would feel better to just tell her everything. But she's a cop.*

"OK. If that's your choice," Nessa said. "So be it. I'm out of here."

She walked out of my house, leaving her full cup of coffee untouched.

What would I do without Nessa? What can I do to fix this?

CHAPTER 19

CHESTER'S TRUTH

I could tell that Chester was suspicious of me ever since the journal incident. He would only meet me if I was with Nessa. He barely looked at me. After a month of this treatment from him, I called and asked him to meet me at the park.

"Hi Chester. This is Carrie."

"Hello," Chester said.

"Hope you're having a nice day," I said.

"Yes."

"Chester, I'm hoping that you will meet me at our favorite spot in the park to talk over a few things." I hoped I didn't sound too desperate.

"Uh, yes. I guess so."

"OK," I said. "How about in an hour?"

"Yes."

It was hard enough to converse with Chester on a good day. I hope this isn't too painful.

Chester was already there when I arrived.

"Hi Chester," I said. "It's good to see you. Thanks for coming." I quickened my step to catch up with him walking in the park.

"What did you want to talk about?"

I should have known he would jump right in. That's Chester's style.

"I, um, um…" I stammered. "Remember that day in the park a while ago when you blurted that 'you saw me'? What did that mean? Where did you see me?"

Chester looked away and watched two dogs romping together.

"Chester?" I asked. "Did you hear my question?"

"Yes," he said. "I'm deciding if I should answer it."

Oh my God. He is so frustrating!

"Why do you have to decide?" I said, putting my hand on his arm to stop him from walking. "Just tell me."

"Fine. All right," Chester said. "I saw you and Danny at the Bronze Lady the night Timmy died."

My whole world seemed to stop in that moment. Hearing him say it aloud was so much worse than just reading his words. My breathing quickened. I could feel the panic attack creeping into my chest. I ran to the rock to sit down and put my head between my knees.

"Carrie?" Chester said, as he followed me to the rock. "Are you OK?"

"I get so upset even thinking about that time," I said.

"Everyone felt upset."

"How could you have seen us there, Chester?" I said, after regaining some control over my breathing. "We were at my house. We told you that."

Chester glanced at me and frowned.

"Why are you bringing this up now, Chester?" I asked. "It was so long ago."

"Because you were there, Carrie. I saw you and Danny running away before I got to the crypt. I saw you!" he screamed.

His raised voice caused me to sit up. I never heard him yell before.

Chester continued. "And I lied to the police, Carrie. Because I care about you. I lied and Jake died."

"Oh, Chester," I said, starting to cry. "It was terrible. But Danny and I were at my house. I swear."

Chester stomped away, never looking back.

The next morning when I returned from my run around the neighborhood, I found another envelope on my porch, addressed to me. I immediately felt my chest tighten but this envelope was clean. This time, I ripped it open as I carried it inside and was surprised to find a note from Chester.

May 6, 1990

Dear Carrie,

You did not tell me the truth yesterday at the park. I know I saw and heard both you and Danny running away from the Bronze Lady that night. Maybe you were at your house before and after, but I know I saw you there. I have kept your secret all these years. I would appreciate it if you would just acknowledge the truth.

Here is a quote I read last night: "The only people I owe my loyalty to are those who never made me questions theirs." I don't know who said it but I understand it now.

I know we have never been best friends but I thought I proved that I could be trusted.

Chester

PS. I also think you have my journal. I can't prove it but it's a strong feeling.

I dropped the letter on the floor and slammed the door on my way out for another run.

After my second but shorter run, I realized I needed to talk with Danny, no matter how scared I felt. I saw him at Clooney's but avoided talking with him except for quick greetings. I called his home and his mother answered.

"Hello?" Mrs. Clooney said.

"Hi, Mrs. Clooney. It's Carrie calling for Danny. Is he at home?"

"Oh, no. He's at work at the bar with his father. How are you, dear girl?"

"I'm just fine, Mrs. Clooney. I miss seeing you."

"We'll just have to do something about that soon. Shall I tell Danny to call you?

"Yes, please. Nice talking with you," I said.

"Goodbye, dear."

Nessa called to tell me she wanted to get some books at the library. I agreed to meet her that afternoon after my volunteer shift. Standing outside waiting for her, I happened to look across the street by a grocery store to see a large camera lens pointed in my direction. The sounds of the expected clicks of the camera were obscured by the constant flow of traffic on the street.

A young man dressed comfortably in jeans and a grey sweatshirt stood behind the lens, partially obscured by a street light. I couldn't make out his facial features due to the navy-blue ball cap pulled down low on his forehead.

Quickly, I glanced around to see who might have been the target. No other people were in our immediate area, except for two who entered the grocery store. Intrigued, I couldn't look away and my mind began racing. Out of the corner of my eye, I spied Nessa parking her car.

He finally moved the camera from his face and started adjusting the lens, still looking down.

Look up at me! I need to see your face.

But again, he brought the lens up and continued shooting in my direction. Frustrated, I ran to meet Nessa at her car and told her, "That man across the street is taking pictures of me."

We looked where I pointed but he was gone. A confused look crossed her face. "What man?"

"I swear, Nessa. I swear I saw someone in a gray sweatshirt and ball cap saying, I think, Syracuse. I just couldn't see the face."

Nessa put her arm around me. "Carrie, I know you've been worried about someone watching you but he was probably just taking pictures of this beautiful library. Come on, let's get some books.

The April day started out gloomy when I called for an emergency session with Nora. She unexpectedly had a cancellation for that afternoon. *How lucky for me.*

After we sat down, Nora commented, "I'm surprised to see you so soon again, Carrie. What's going on?"

"I had a very eventful week," I said. "Thank you for fitting me in."

Nora tilted her head to study me and nodded, encouraging me to start.

"Someone," I said, "a man I don't know, is kind of stalking me."

"Kind of stalking?" Nora asked. "How often?"

"Before our last session, there were at least three times," I said. "This past week? Twice already. Does that sound like stalking?"

"That sounds like a lot. Tell me what you are experiencing."

"It started with a car following me during my runs," I started. "The windows were darkened so I couldn't see anyone."

"Is it possible the car belongs to a neighbor?" Nora said.

I thought for a moment. "I guess so but I saw the same car in Plattsburgh. That was the first time."

"Have you ever seen his face?" Nora asked.

"Yes. I've seen him twice since the darkened car. It is not anybody I know." *But he might be related to someone I know.*

"When and where did you see him?"

I struggled to feel comfortable in my seat, taking off my shoes and tucking my feet under my legs. "I saw him once peeping in my window at home and another time in a crowd at a concert. I was terrified when I saw his face."

I watched as Nora scribbled her notes. "There have been quite a few studies done about the feeling of being watched," she said. "Your gut about being followed may be right, but can be wrong. Tell me more about how you feel when it's happening."

"When he looks directly at me, I'm frightened. Actually, the second time I remember my neck stiffened and my body tingled."

"That's understandable, Carrie. Our amygdala is the part of the brain that prompts our sense of fear. It also handles facial recognition. So that makes a lot of sense that you feel threatened."

"I do," I said. "He smirked the last time he stared at me."

"A direct gaze can signal a threat or a desire to dominate a person," Nora said. "It's important that you pay attention to your surroundings and keep calm. Are you practicing visualization regularly?"

"Yes," I nodded. 'It's working much better after your help."

"You know, Carrie, if the stalking continues, you might think about reporting it to the police, just as a precaution. Maybe they can find out who he is. I do feel relieved that he hasn't confronted you."

"What would I do if he did confront me?" I asked.

"Perhaps you should always try to have someone in your company," said Nora. "Do you know anyone else in your neighborhood who runs? Perhaps you could run in a more public setting?"

"All right. I don't really know any of my neighbors but I can try the different setting idea."

"Good, Carrie. Do you feel better having shared that with me?" Nora asked as she stood up.

"Yes," I said, nodding.

CHAPTER 20

A FLOOD OF MEMORIES

My phone rang the next morning, the first of May, just as I grasped the doorknob to leave and run errands. The weatherman forecast a lovely day in the 70s, unusually warm for an early morning in May.

"Hello?" I said.

"Hi Carrie. It's Danny."

He didn't need to identify himself. I would know his voice anywhere.

"Uh, hi," I stammered.

"Carrie, Ma said you called. I've seen you around and it's just too strange feeling like I can't talk with you. Would it be too upsetting for us to meet?"

Can I do that? Can I talk with him?

"Thinking we could meet in Webber Park today by the stone wall," Danny said, "if it's not covered with too much moss." He laughed. "Around 10:30?"

He's laughing? What the hell?

"Carrie, what do you think?"

"I guess so," I said. "I'll see you there."

I couldn't get off the phone fast enough. Fortunately, I only had a couple of hours before our meeting so I busied myself around the house until I started my walk to the park.

I hadn't been alone with Danny since 1970. I still felt emotionally drawn to him and I wondered if I would still be attracted to him physically.

Twenty minutes later and waiting at the wall, I examined my nails. I had recently started getting my nails done in an effort to stop biting them down to the quick. That seemed to be working but my hangnails were always there to pick.

"Hi, Carrie."

I hadn't heard Danny approach, so deep in my thoughts. Looking up at his face, the flood of memories almost overwhelmed me.

He sat down next to me on the stone wall. "Were we really together only three and a half years?" he asked.

"Yes," I said. "They were intense times."

"They sure were."

"Have you thought about all we did?" I glanced at him.

"All the time. Sometimes it seems like yesterday."

I turned my body to look at him. "Have you felt like you were constantly looking over your shoulder since then?"

"Used to freak me out," Danny nodded. "We had to grow up really fast."

Now that I had started, I couldn't seem to stop talking. "Where did you go after the war? Why didn't you come back for me?"

"I wanted to, Carrie. At least in the beginning." He stared up at the trees. "But after I left Nam and decompressed a bit in California, I decided you were better off without me because of all of our secrets."

My body started to shake as I swiped my tears from my face. "It was hard enough to hold one secret but two has been almost impossible by myself. I hated you for doing that to me. Those damned secrets wanted to seep out of my pores but I knew I had to keep them under my skin."

"I know how you feel," said Danny. "We have so much history, Carrie. It's as scary as the war was. I can say that with certainty."

"So you stayed in California?" I asked. "Why didn't you come back here?"

Danny turned away from me and sighed. "I got pretty messed up in Nam."

"I worried so much for you," I said. "What happened?"

"You can only see so many people die in front of you before you become used to it," he admitted. "That and my guilt. Guilt about Jake. Timmy. You. I couldn't face all of those demons anymore and starting using big time."

"Using? I asked. "Like drugs?"

"Exactly," he said. "That's when I stopped writing to you. I didn't think I could write a coherent letter without you realizing. So I just stopped. I'm so sorry." He rubbed the top of my hand.

He stopped writing because of that, not me.

"You're fine now, right?" I asked. "When did that happen?"

"This part is really sad. I started hanging out with another addict in San Francisco. Misery loves company, right?" Danny stood up and started to pace.

I nodded slightly, frowning.

"We were both doing heroin and pills. She overdosed. When I found her, I happened to be between hits and I walked right to a church and asked for help. Scared the living shit out of me."

"Oh, that's horrible. Then what happened?"

"The priest at the church brought me to a clinic. Turns out it serviced all guys returning from Nam. What a bunch we were," Danny said, shaking his head. "Damaged goods."

Danny stood up to pace. "I was there for ninety days. It was hell but I've never looked back."

"Kudos to you, Danny," I said. "Amazing you came through on the other side. I'm glad you did."

Danny bent down to hug me. "Thanks, Carrie. It's nice to hear that from you."

"I think I need you in my life, Danny," I said. "To talk with. Share these overwhelming fears and memories. Would you do that for me?"

"Yeah. I would like that, Carrie. I need someone to share these feelings of guilt with also." Danny sat back down next to me. "Looks like I'll be staying here working as a bartender at Clooney's, of course. I never went back to school. Glad to see that you did."

"Teaching proved to be a great distraction," I said. "And I run. I run hoping the sweat will wash away my guilt, even if a little at a time? I've been running for twenty God-dammed years! Aren't I clean and clear yet?"

Danny put his arm around my shoulder and squeezed, ever so slightly.

Oh, my God, his touch still makes me melt!

"I'm impressed that you are so active," he said. "You look great."

"Thanks for that, Danny," I said. We sat for a moment lost in our own thoughts. "Hey, would you meet me at the Bronze Lady tomorrow morning at 10:30?"

Danny sat up straight. "Sure, but why?"

"We have some unfinished business there." *Something I had been thinking about for a while.*

I stood up to leave, but Danny grabbed my hand to turn me around to face him.

"Thanks for coming, Carrie. I missed you."

I missed you too, Danny. I could see the Danny I had loved. I could feel it.

The next morning, I made a quick stop before I met Danny at the Bronze Lady. It was surreal walking there from my house, just like high school. Because of all the brush around the statue, I didn't realize that Danny was there until I entered the small courtyard.

"Oh!" I said. "You're here already. Good."

Danny gestured toward my right hand. "Wha'cha got there?"

I held up my quick stop purchase. "Flowers."

"For me?" Danny asked.

"No, not for you." I smiled and shook my head.

Danny looked around. "Is someone else coming to meet us?"

"No." I reached down to pull him up from his seated position. "I thought we should bring the Lady flowers in memory of Jake and Timmy."

"That's really thoughtful, Carrie. We never took any time to mourn them."

I laid the bouquet of roses, alstroemeria, and baby's breath across the Lady's hands. I stepped back to enjoy how she seemed to cradle the flowers.

"How about a moment of silence?" I asked, looking up at Danny.

"I agree," he said, as he lowered his head.

After a few minutes, Danny spoke up. "Carrie, I've been wondering about something since our talk yesterday. Did you have any other relationships in Plattsburgh?"

"Just a few. I waited about a year to hear from you. Then a high school Social Studies teacher asked me out three times, but I just didn't see it happening. Then, a parent actually set me up with her husband's friend but—," I shrugged. "I honestly needed to protect myself."

"I know exactly what you mean," Danny agreed. "I never wanted anyone too close."

Suddenly, the little courtyard seemed stifling.

"Better get going, Danny," I said.

"Have a good day," he said as he walked toward his car. "Hey, want a ride?"

"Sure. Thanks."

As soon as I arrived home, I put on my running shoes and started to jog my usual route until—once again, something stopped me in my tracks. Perhaps, I was getting closer to feeling like I didn't have to escape. This time, I could sprint toward something, to someone. Maybe to Danny.

CHAPTER 21

THE STALKER REVEALED

By June 1990, I could tell my talks with Danny and Nora were helping me to feel better. Nessa still suspected I had secrets but she felt relief that I could talk to Danny without getting hysterical. Chester still never engaged with me but Danny, Nessa, Chester, and I were a foursome, spending a lot of time together at Clooney's. And I was still drinking.

I, however, still had the stalker. I finally opened up to the group at Clooney's one very hot afternoon. Actually, Nessa brought him up.

"So, Carrie, are you going to tell them about your stalker?" she asked.

"What are you talking about Nessa?" Danny blurted. "What the hell, Carrie?"

Even Chester expressed his anger. For the first time in a long while, he looked at me and said, "I cannot believe you haven't told us."

I looked around the table. "I don't see how any of you could help," I said. "I have no idea who he is. He just shows up at random times, usually when I'm alone. I feel like I'm going crazy."

"Why would someone stalk you?" asked Chester.

"No idea," I said.

I sat across the table from Danny and lightly nudged his leg. He glanced up at me and his eyes grew very large, but he stayed silent.

Nessa broke the silence. "I suggested she go to the police department and register a complaint."

"Let us know if it gets bad, Carrie," said Danny. "OK? None of us want anyone bothering you."

Heads nodded in agreement and everyone started to leave. Nessa grabbed my arm on the way out and told me, "We are going to the police station right now. You can tell them what you know and get it in the record."

"But," I started to protest.

"Carrie," Nessa said in her cop voice, "we are going."

We headed to the police station and I talked with an officer. Somehow, I avoided questions about any familiarity.

"Thanks for making me go, Nessa," I said. "I feel better that something's in the record now."

"Cops are your friends," she said, laughing. I had to laugh too, even though I was petrified I had just been in the police station.

My phone rang as I walked in the door. I ran to pick it up and I heard Danny say, "You didn't think you should have told me about this stalker guy?"

"Well, hello to you, too," I said. "I don't know, Danny. We definitely need to talk about this, and soon. I have some frightening thoughts."

"I guess you would."

"Can you come over for dinner tomorrow night?" I asked.

Danny paused. "I think I'm working but I'll just ask Dad to change with me. I doubt they have plans."

"Great. Thanks," I said. "See you around 7."

"I'll be there."

The doorbell rang at 7:05 pm, causing my stomach to flutter. I opened the door to see Danny grinning while holding a small bouquet of daisies.

"You remembered my favorite," I said with a smile. "I hope those are for me!"

"Of course," he said.

Danny followed me to the kitchen to get a vase. I saw him glance into the living room on the way.

"Wow," Danny said. "It's been a long time since I've been in this house. I can see you've changed some things, like the TV."

"Yes, definitely an essential new buy!" We laughed. "Let's sit in the dining room and I'll get dinner on the table."

I had cooked Danny's favorite, pork chops with mashed potatoes, glazed carrots, and applesauce. He nodded and smiled as I placed his plate in front of him. I set down a beer for him and one for me.

"Well," he said. "This is a special night." He dug into his plate.

After a few minutes of small talk, he asked about the stalker.

"Danny, there's so much I need to tell you. I'm almost afraid to start."

"Come on, Carrie," he said. "You know you can tell me."

"Yeah, I do." I looked across the table and sighed deeply. "Give me a minute."

I stood up, cleared the dinner plates, and brought them to the kitchen. Danny leaned forward as I returned and sat down.

"Carrie?"

"Here goes. It really started when I was in Plattsburgh last year after my parents died. I felt someone in a dark car following me during my run. Just a scary feeling."

"Did you see the person?" Danny said.

"No, but the same car followed me again when I took my run in this neighborhood. That's when I started getting worried."

Danny's forehead became wrinkled. "Hmm. That is strange."

"But the absolutely worst thing happened when I saw a face in the window after getting these on my doorstep." I went to the buffet and picked up the envelopes and dropped them next to his plate.

I gave him a few minutes to read and absorb the letters.

"But, Carrie—"

"I know," I said. "Jake is dead."

"Then how the hell?"

"Wait, Danny, the face I saw in the window looked exactly like Jake!"

"Are you sure you saw someone? These letters are creepy. Maybe—"

"Yes!" I said, a bit too loud. "I even ran out to ask the landscaper to confirm that someone had been there."

"OK," Danny said. "Let's assume it's the same guy in the car. Any ideas?"

"Here's the thing. This time I saw his face. After that I saw him at a concert watching me. But he disappeared before I could confront him."

"Now it does sound like someone is definitely stalking you," Danny said. "But who, and why?"

"This is the part I'm afraid to tell you," I said, my eyes welling up.

"Carrie, what is it?"

"Nessa and I were talking about this guy and how much he looked like Jake, which of course is impossible. But then Nessa asked if Jake had any cousins. But why would they bother me? Then, she said, Jake and Timmy didn't have any children. That's when I freaked out."

Danny leaned on his fist and looked away. "Because they died before they had kids?'

I took a deep breath and let it out. "Because—maybe our baby was Timmy's."

"No!" Danny pushed away from the table and left the house.

The next afternoon when I returned from a baby shower for another library volunteer, I saw something taped to my door. The note read, "MEET ME AT THE BRONZE LADY AT 7 PM ON THURSDAY NIGHT." The same block printing as the postcard. I called Danny.

As soon as he picked up the phone, I yelled, "Danny! Thank God you answered."

"I'm not ready to talk about this yet, Carrie," he said.

"I got a note from the stalker!"

"What?"

"I found it taped to my front door. He wants to meet me."

"When?"

"Tonight. I know you're probably still upset but I need you to come with me."

"Where?" he said. "What time?"

"Seven o'clock. At the Bronze Lady.

"It's ten to seven right now, Carrie. I'll meet you there. Nessa's here. I'll bring her."

I put on my running shoes and flew out of the house. The leaves on the ground were a bit slippery from the rain that morning. I ran in the middle of the road and crossed the street into the cemetery. It was eerily quiet as I wound my way over to the Lady. I slowed down as I approached.

Should I wait for Danny? What if the stalker has a gun?

Making a quick decision to just go ahead, I entered the small area and a tall, thin young man with dark hair turned to face me. I gasped. Just as I thought, he looked like a combination of Jake and Timmy. Definitely related.

"At last we meet, Carolyn Peters," he said.

"Who are you?" I asked. "Why have you been tormenting me?"

"Oh, good. That's what I wanted to do. Torment you."

"But why? What have I done to you?"

He smirked. "Does the date February 28, 1968 mean anything to you?"

I gasped again and covered my mouth with my hand. "How would you know that?"

"It's my birthdate, Mom."

I felt my knees start to buckle when someone caught me.

"Carrie, it's Danny. Nessa's here too."

"Oh, Danny, it's him. It's him."

"Well, there's my supposed Dad," the man said. "And, Mom, is this Nessa, your best friend?"

I glanced at Nessa. She raised her hands in a questioning pose. "What is he talking about?" Nessa asked. "Why is he calling you Mom and Dad?"

"Wait, Nessa," said Danny, pointing at the man. "How did you find us? What is your name?"

"My name is Keith Devlin. This will be a long story. Maybe you want to sit down?"

"Just get on with it," Danny said, still bracing me.

"Your choice," Keith said as he sat on the edge of the crypt. "Like I was telling Mom, I was born on February 28, 1968 in Plattsburgh, New York and immediately put up for adoption. My adoptive parents explained all of this to me about three years ago when I started asking questions. I didn't look like either of them. They are both very fair and, well, I'm obviously darker. They were great parents. I'm an only child but I never knew the rest of their family. They kept me all to themselves."

"Where did you grow up?" I asked. Now that I suspected he really was my child, I wanted to know everything.

"In the Albany area."

That would explain the postcard and its postmark.

"Why did you call me your supposed dad?" Danny asked.

"The birth certificate bears your name. Then, adoption through Catholic Charities. All this sound familiar?"

Danny and I nodded.

"But how did you find us?" said Danny.

"I just went to Plattsburgh and looked in the phone book," said Keith. "It was almost too easy. Then, after you moved, I asked the people in your house where you had gone. They were so nice and told me about your move back to Sleepy Hollow."

"Wow," I said, moving closer to Danny.

"I started figuring this mystery out after I visited your family tavern, Dad."

"What?" we both said at the same time.

"Yeah, I sat in the next booth when your other friend, Chester, talked about the pictures on the walls. How they were so interesting because they showed the history of the town, including one group of pictures from the twentieth celebration of the place in 1967. I looked very closely at a picture with all of you in it, including two guys I didn't know but who looked shockingly like me."

I squeezed Danny's hand as I began to swoon. Danny helped me to sit down. Nessa remained standing to the side.

"When you all left the tavern that day, I asked Mr. Clooney about the picture. He identified everyone and told me the sad story about Jake and Timmy's family. He also said, 'Funny, you actually look a bit like those boys.'"

Nessa had waited long enough. "I want to know why you are bothering my best friend!"

Keith smiled condescendingly at her. "I'm getting to that, Mija. You'll soon find out."

"What?" Nessa said as she took two steps toward Keith.

"I am here to find out about my father," Keith said. "Mr. Clooney told me that Jake and Timmy's father died of Huntington's Disease."

Danny said, "So what does that have to do with me?"

Keith took a step toward us. "I have Juvenile Huntington's disease," Keith said, as he looked deeply into my eyes. "And, I'm pissed."

"Oh, no. I am so sorry," I said. "That's not what I hoped for you."

"Is that why you gave me away?" Keith said. "That possibility?"

"No, never," I said. Both Danny and I shook our heads. "We were young and unmarried. We did what we thought was best for you."

Keith harrumphed. "So, Mom, Jake or Timmy?"

I spoke up. "I never slept with anyone else except Danny, until—"

"Until you didn't?" Keith said. "That's convenient."

"It wasn't like that!" I mumbled.

"Sure," Keith said.

"You don't understand. Timmy raped me!" I blurted, burying my head into Danny's chest.

Keith's jaw dropped.

I heard Nessa gulping for air and then choking. "Oh, Carrie," she said.

"Raped?" asked Keith, almost whispering.

And before we could reply, he ran away toward the cemetery exit.

"Oh, no!" I said. "Where did he go, Danny? What if we never see him again?"

Danny and Nessa both hugged me, trying to comfort me.

Nessa was the first to speak. "Well, that was quite unexpected. I have so many questions but I'll wait and call you in the morning."

Danny nodded. "Come on Carrie. Let's get you home.

It was a long night of tossing and turning.

Keith called the next morning to ask that we all meet again at the Lady. Danny, Nessa, and I agreed to meet him before Nessa's shift started at 3 pm.

It had rained early that morning and we walked carefully to avoid the dripping branches and soggy grass. Keith was waiting for us, pacing between the statue and the crypt.

We greeted each other with quick waves and I was surprised when Nessa started the conversation.

"I have a question, Keith," she said. "One of many, but I'll start with this one. Why did you want to meet here at the Bronze Lady?"

Danny put his arm around me as I shivered.

"Mr. Clooney told me this was where Timmy died, and that Jake was convicted for it," Keith said. "I thought it might be appropriate."

"The Lady brings up many sad memories for us," I said.

After a minute, Danny said, "Carrie never told anyone about the rape or the baby except me, Keith. She carried this secret for a long time. Even Nessa didn't now. Our families didn't either."

"Do you understand why I wanted you to be Danny's?" I asked. "Honestly, I never thought of the possibility you weren't until I saw you in my window."

"Sorry, but I need a few minutes," Keith said. He walked around the crypt and started to speak as he came around to the front.

"I am embarrassed. Honestly, I am so sorry I've been tormenting you, so consumed with anger and fear of this disease."

We all stood quietly trying to absorb the last ten minutes. Danny broke the silence.

"Carrie, I need to apologize for my reaction to Keith possibly being Timmy's. I was unfair." He leaned over to hug me and I felt we were alone in that moment, just me and Danny again.

"So, where do we go from here?" Keith said. "Nessa, are you going to arrest me for stalking?"

"Not unless Carrie wants to press charges," she said.

I shook my head adamantly. "Absolutely not, unless Keith is going to continue to torment me."

"No," Keith said, shaking his head. "I'm done with that. I hope you accept my apology."

I squeezed Danny's hand. "Danny, what do you think? Should we plan a dinner tomorrow night for the three of us? I think we have a lot to talk about."

"Yes," Danny said, looking at Keith. "I've always thought of you as my child. It would be great to hear about your life."

Keith approached Danny to shake Danny's hand. "Absolutely," he said. "I hope you're a good cook, Carrie. Can I call you that?"

I laughed and said, "My heart is going to burst! Can I give you a hug, Keith?"

"Sure."

As I embraced this young man who had grown so tall without me, I knew we were starting a new life. Friends. Maybe mother and son.

I woke up the next morning feeling renewed. Yes, that other nagging secret still lingered but today, I had something that made me smile. No, not something. Someone. Tonight, Danny and I would find out all about the child we thought we shared, about his life and the people who raised him.

On my run that morning, I knew that I could run without fear of someone following me, wanting nothing more than to torment me. I ran down to Kingsland Point, that special spot on the Hudson where I swam as a kid, ignorant of pollution later discovered in the water. The expanse of the river looked to be the widest in this spot and I thought of the early natives and the Dutch who had boated there, on their way to find new places and opportunities.

What a beautiful river! Aren't I lucky to live here?

I honestly felt lighter and enjoyed the crisp morning air and beautiful blue sky I saw on the run back to my house. I smiled and greeted my older neighbors walking their two golden labs.

"Have a nice day!" I called to them.

Turning the key in my door, I could hear my phone start to ring. I quickly reached it and picked it up just as the caller hung up.

Darn. I hope no one is cancelling for tonight.

The phone rang again just as I placed it back on the receiver. "Hello," I said.

"Hi Mija." Although I loved hearing Nessa's voice, I knew I had a lot of explaining to do.

"Carrie, what the hell happened? Wow. That's some story."

"Nessa, are you working today? Can we meet?"

"I actually have a late shift today so I'm free until 3," she said.

"I'm prepping for dinner tonight," I said. "Can you come over here in about an hour?"

"Perfect. See you then."

As we hung up, I realized I no longer had to keep that secret from Nessa. My solid best friend. I couldn't wait to hug her.

I worked in the kitchen preparing an apple pie that I would serve with vanilla ice cream.

Who wouldn't like this? Yum.

I turned on the radio and moved my hips and feet to "Straight Up". *Wish I could move like Paula Abdul.* "Ha!" I laughed out loud.

When the doorbell rang, my body stiffened with the anticipation of explaining so much to Nessa. After our hug, we walked into the kitchen and I headed straight to the counter to work on the dough for the pie crust.

"I am so sorry for not telling you," I said, my back to her. "As a rape victim, I felt helpless, hopeless. And at fault. Like, my fault for being drunk, my fault for getting into—"

"Wait a minute, Carrie. Start from the beginning."

I turned around and sat down at the table with her. "You know how much I drank after Danny broke up with me?"

Nessa nodded, her eyes growing large.

"At the party after prom, Greg left me to be with his friends and you and Jake looked happy so I just decided to walk home. I know," I said, raising my hand to stop her as she started to interrupt. "Bad idea. I must have been thinking about Danny because when a car drove up next to me and asked if I wanted a ride, Danny was all I could see and hear."

"And you willingly went into someone's car?" Nessa said. "Timmy's, I'm assuming?"

"Yes, but I must have passed out because I didn't realize it wasn't Danny until I woke up to Timmy raping me. Oh, Nessa." I dropped my head into my hands.

"That fucker," Nessa said.

"That's exactly what Danny called him."

"I never understood his meanness," Nessa said, shaking her head and looking out the window. "I can't help but think you weren't the only girl he raped."

"I don't know," I said. "He dropped me at my house and then began to torment me at school by whispering things in my ear."

"Fucker."

"Almost as bad as the rape. I felt totally violated and I couldn't tell anyone."

"Wait a minute. Is that why you freaked out that day in school and I took you to the Nurse's Office?" Nessa asked.

"Yes. I told Danny that day after school and then Timmy died that night."

"Do you think that's what Timmy and Jake argued about at The Bronze Lady?"

"Maybe," I said, avoiding her eyes and returning to the counter to work on the pie crust.

"That makes total sense," said Nessa. "I couldn't figure out what would have made Jake so angry to fight with Timmy."

Grimacing, I finished rolling the dough and lightly placed it in the pie dish.

"I'm glad you finally shared the truth with me," Nessa said. "Sorry to run but I've gotta get ready for work."

"OK," I said, as we walked to the door and shared a hug. "I'll call you tomorrow. Wish me luck tonight!"

"Always, Mija," she said, blowing me a kiss.

The table looked beautiful, set with my mother's best placemats and napkins in the color scheme of brown and orange for the fall. Only three place settings. For the little family I hoped would show up for dinner.

Danny arrived first, bearing a bouquet of yellow mums and baby's breath. Almost like he knew what colors I would choose for the table.

"Hi, Carrie," he said, handing me the flowers. "Keith here yet?"

"No, you're the first," I said. "What can I get you to drink?"

"Do you have any beer?"

"Yes," I said, with a smile. "I knew you were coming."

I brought his beer to the dining table as the doorbell rang.

"Hi Keith, come on in," I said, as I opened the door.

"Thanks," he said, stumbling over the door frame.

"Ooh. You, OK?" I asked.

"Yeah, just a little clumsy sometimes," Keith admitted. "I brought this bottle of white wine. Hope you like it."

"I love white wine," I said. "Very thoughtful."

I led Keith into the dining room where Danny stood to shake his hand. When I asked what he wanted to drink, Keith also asked for a beer. After getting a beer out of the refrigerator, I poured myself a glass of the white wine. Taking a deep breath, I walked back into the dining room, where my two special men were each sitting at the ends of the table. I heard Danny asking Keith if he went to college.

"Yes," Keith said. "I went to State University of New York at Albany and studied Secondary Education to teach History."

"I'm a teacher," I said. "But elementary. I'm going to the kitchen for our dinner. Don't say anything while I'm gone."

Keith smiled at me. "Yes, ma'am!" he said.

As I carried the food in and placed the plates in front of them, Danny couldn't wait any longer.

"You're pretty young Keith," Danny said. "Just out of school?"

"Yes," Keith said. "I graduated early last December. But I haven't taught yet. My dad died two years ago of cancer and left me some money. That's what I've been living off since then."

"Where are you living?" I asked.

"I have an apartment in Ossining, about twenty minutes from here."

"Keith," I said. "I have so many questions to ask you. I almost don't know where to start."

Danny jumped in to help me. "So," he said. "What do you think about what happened last night?"

Keith sat up straight in his chair. "I have been really pissed off for quite a while because I didn't have all the information. My mother really had to struggle to get a copy of the birth certificate. Apparently, she knows someone in the Diocese in Albany. I felt hurt and very confused about being given up."

Keith's arm jerked, I think involuntarily. Danny and I glanced at each other and he reached for my hand.

"I did manage to graduate college but I struggled my last year," Keith explained. "I felt depressed and very irritable. My mother became concerned, of course, and sent me to her doctor for a complete checkup. But the doctor felt more concern about my stumbling during track practice and these stupid involuntary jerks. He ordered an MRI of my brain."

"What exactly is Huntington's?" asked Danny, between bites.

Keith took a sip of his beer. "It's a progressive disorder that causes the breakdown of brain cells in certain areas of the brain. Actually, lucky me, I have Juvenile Huntington's, which gives me a shorter life expectancy of ten years."

I gasped and put my hand over my mouth to push the air back in. *Only ten years?* I suddenly lost my appetite but took a long drink of my wine.

"When I heard that Timmy and Jake's father died of Huntington's," Keith said. "I knew one of them had to be my father. This disease does not skip generations. I guess Timmy must have died before he got it."

"I can't imagine how you've dealt with this news," Danny said. "How did you find out about Jake and Timmy?"

"Remember I told you that your dad mentioned that I resembled them?" Keith asked. "I actually told your dad I had been adopted and was looking for connections here in town. Your dad, such a nice guy, remembered he had a box that Jake's mother had given him before she died. The box held things that belonged to Jake."

"My dad mentioned the box to me," said Danny, "but I haven't been able to deal with Jake's memory."

"He suggested I take a look through the box," Keith continued, "to see if anything made sense. I couldn't believe my luck. I told him I'd return the box, which I did after I took out the old letter he had tried to send to you."

I was speechless.

"Damn him. Damn Timmy!" Keith suddenly stood up and yelled. "Why did he have to rape you? I shouldn't have been born!" Keith threw his beer glass across the room.

"Oh, no," I stood up, shocked. "Danny?"

Danny walked over to Keith and gently put his arm around him. "Let's go outside for a short walk, Keith," Danny said.

As they left, I called behind them, "It's fine, Keith. Don't worry." I went to the kitchen for a sponge, mop, and bucket to clean up the broken glass. I also cleared away the dinner plates and started the coffee for dessert.

Keith and Danny came back to the house about fifteen minutes later. The apple pie, ice cream, and coffee were already on the table.

Keith spoke first. "Carrie, please accept my apology. Did I break anything?"

"No, just the beer bottle," I smiled. "But I have another for you."

Keith hung his head. *Oh, he's embarrassed.*

"I'm going to help Keith explain what happened," Danny said. "Is that OK, Keith?"

Keith nodded.

"Apparently, that type of compulsive behavior is a symptom of the disease," explained Danny.

"I also have a lot of episodes of anxiety and depression," Keith said.

I thought for a moment. "Keith," I said, "do you have a good doctor down here?"

"I go back to Albany to see the doctor who first diagnosed me," Keith said. "I feel confident with him."

I hesitated before asking the next question.

"What, Carrie?" said Danny. "Just ask."

"Do you see a psychiatrist or psychologist?"

"Not yet," said Keith.

"I see a wonderful psychologist for anxiety," I said.

Keith leaned his chin on his hand and focused on me.

I continued. "I think you might need to see a psychiatrist in case you need some medication. I can ask her if she knows someone, if you like."

"I think so," said Keith. "Let's talk again about that. I would like to ask my regular doctor and my mom about that first."

"Sounds good. I'll ask her for a name in case you become ready for one."

We all finished eating our pie and taking sips of coffee, quiet in our thoughts until Danny spoke up. "I think Carrie and I are most concerned that you understand we gave you up for adoption out of love. I honestly always thought you were mine."

I reached out to touch Keith's arm. "I hope you will keep in touch, Keith. I would very much like to get to know you better."

"Me, too," Keith said as he reached into his shirt pocket and pulled out two small slips of paper. "Here's my phone number and address. Call me anytime."

Danny laughed. "You may be sorry you did that, Keith!"

We all hugged at the door as I watched them walk together to their cars.

My two favorite men. I hope I can sleep tonight. What an amazing evening.

The next day, rain and cold changed plans to hike at the Rockefeller Estate with Nessa again. Instead, we went to Clooney's to share lunch. Nessa lit up a cigarette.

"I can't even tell you how good it feels to talk with you about that secret," I said, grabbing and squeezing her hand. "I really have no idea why I didn't tell you. You've always been my best friend."

Nessa nodded. "I don't understand either, Mija," she said. "But that's water under the dam. How did dinner go last night?"

Just then, Mr. Clooney showed up with a free plate of appetizers for us. He squeezed my shoulder and patted my back.

I smiled up at him and said, "This is nice. Thanks."

Mr. Clooney moved on to the next table. Turning back to Nessa, I said, "Keith shared about the Huntington's diagnosis and we actually saw some of his symptoms. Poor guy."

"Symptoms?" Nessa said. "Like what?"

"He has some clumsiness, which showed up when he stumbled over the door frame. He also had an episode of compulsive behavior. Very unexpected when he shouted, 'Damn Timmy! Why did he have to rape you?'"

Nessa's eyes grew round. "What did you do?" she asked.

"Danny took him outside to cool down," I said. "You know, Nessa, Danny would have been a great father." I looked over at Mr. Clooney tending the bar, towel over his shoulder. "And he," tilting my head in his direction, "would have been a terrific grandfather." I picked at a hangnail.

"Good to hear Keith's rounded a corner about you and Danny," she said.

"And, he gave us his phone number," I said, starting to bounce in my seat. "He had them all ready to give us on two little slips of paper."

"That's amazing, Mija," Nessa said, putting out her cigarette in the ashtray. She immediately took out her pack of Camels, her brand since high school, and lit up another one.

I raised my eyebrows and said, "Why don't you take a break with the cigs, Nessa? I've noticed that you're chain smoking now."

"Hey," she said. "this is my only vice, right?" She paused to look at me. "No worse that picking at and biting your nails."

"Truer words were never spoken," I said, raising my glass to toast.

Two days later, I ran up the steps to Nora's office feeling giddy to tell her my news. As she opened the door, I grabbed and hugged her, almost catching her off balance.

"Oh, my," said Nora. "Nice to see you too!"

As I hurried to sit down, I said, "I have such good news. A secret finally revealed."

"Let's start then," she said, nestling into her chair.

I told Nora about the rape, the baby, and the adoption. I paused to take a breath and then finished the story about the Huntington's Disease and Timmy being the father.

"Whew," I said. I took a sip of water that Nora always had ready for me. "Keith felt sorry for tormenting me and agreed to come to dinner the next night with Danny and me. We had a nice time and Keith shared a lot about the Huntington's."

"That's quite a bit of news to take in all at once," she said, putting down her pen. "And, a huge secret to keep. No wonder you felt overwhelmed. Are you going to continue your relationship with Keith?"

"That's the best part," I said. "He gave us his phone number. I still can hardly contain my excitement!"

"It's no wonder you are so happy, Carrie," said Nora. "Looks like our time is up for today. I hope to continue this talk next time. Same time?"

"Yes, but in one week, not two. I have more to share, if you can believe it."

"I believe it, Carrie. See you then."

I left Nora's office and felt like I floated down the stairs. Telling secrets can be good for the soul.

CHAPTER 22

A BEST FRIEND
IN TROUBLE

"There goes that damned pager again," I growled.

Nessa and I had just shared a great pizza and were window shopping on North Broadway when I heard the dreaded buzz. I tried my best not to give Nessa my impatient look. After all, it was her job.

"Gotta go! It's right around the corner on Neperan. Can you get home?" she yelled over her shoulder as she ran toward her parked car. "Gotta stop at the car!"

I followed her, saw her get her gun, holster it and turn back to Neperan Road. Instead of leaving to walk home, I ran after her.

Angry voices reached my ears as I rounded the corner. I came abruptly to a stop when I spotted a man and a woman on the sidewalk. The man held the woman in a choke hold, waved a gun, and yelled obscenities. The way he lurched made me think he'd had way too much to drink. I couldn't tell if he was standing on his own behind her or if her weight supported him. Nessa drew her gun, pointed, and called out a warning to them.

Two more police cars sped up to the scene and screeched to a stop, lights flashing. They were temporary distractions for me as I could not take my eyes off Nessa. I could not hear what Nessa was saying to the man and woman but the man's voice escalated as the woman struggled to get away.

Suddenly, the sound of a gunshot filled the air. I hit the ground. A woman screamed and policemen yelled. Then, two more shots. I looked up and saw the woman, now splattered in blood, standing by herself, shaking and screaming. The man lay at her feet, unmoving. But where was Nessa? I couldn't see Nessa.

I heard a call to 911. "Officer down! Officer down! Send ambulance to South Neperan."

"No!" I yelled and I sprinted to the scene where Nessa was laying on the ground bleeding. "Nessa!"

"Stay back, Miss, "the policeman ordered. "She's alive. Help is coming. Oh, this is Nando's kid!" He yelled to the other policeman at the car. "Page Nando and tell him to meet us at the hospital!"

"I'm her best friend! Let me stay with her," I pleaded.

The medics allowed me to ride in the ambulance with Nessa. I could not take my eyes off her, almost willing her to open her eyes to look at me. But she was covered in tubes, blankets, and a breathing mask.

My world had changed in a split second. Nessa had always been there when I needed her. There to give a smart retort or a tight hug to calm my body and mind down. Would I be able to come through for her?

I called Danny as soon as we arrived at Phelps Memorial Hospital. Nando bustled by me to talk with the doctor. He came back, took me by the arm, and led me to a chair next to Nessa's mother, who was silently saying the Rosary. I hugged her as tightly as I could before I sat down. She noticed my tears and gave me a few tissues.

Nando shared what he knew. "Nessa got shot and the bullet exited her upper arm. Right now, they're just cleaning her up. I don't even think she needs surgery, Mama." He put his hand on his wife's leg and squeezed.

"Gracias, Dios, por todas tus bendiciones," Nessa's mother said, crossing herself.

"Aye, mi amor," Nando said, leaning over to kiss her on the cheek.

I just love them so much. I hate to see them sad.

Just then, a heavy-set man in a white coat approached us. "Are you Nessa Martinez's family?" he asked.

When we nodded, he continued. "I am Dr. Heinz, the attending physician. "Nessa had a perforating gunshot wound in her upper left arm."

I spoke up. "What does 'perforating' mean?"

"It means that the bullet entered and exited her body so no surgery is needed at this point. There was a lot of blood loss at the exit wound, which is normal. She is a lucky woman. The bullet missed her artery. We would like to keep her overnight tonight to monitor her but, barring any infection, she should be ready to go back to work in two to three weeks. Any questions?"

Nando interpreted for his wife and then listened to his wife's question. "When can we see her, Dr. Heinz?"

"The nurse will come out to tell you when Nessa can have visitors." He turned and walked back into another patient's room.

The three of us held hands and smiled with relief.

I stayed until after Nessa's parents were able to visit with her. When they left the room, Nando hugged me and said, "She's pretty tired, Carrie. The nurse said you could see her but only for a few minutes." *That's all I need.*

I quietly opened the door and gasped seeing Nessa looking so helpless. Nessa, my confident, only afraid of a gunshot wound friend, had all kinds of tubes and IVs connecting her body to monitors. Her eyes were closed. I gently touched her hand. She opened her eyes slowly and grimaced in pain.

"Hi, Nessa," I whispered. "How's my kick-ass best friend?"

Nessa struggled to smile and slurred her words a bit as she answered. "Not so kick-ass right now."

"Are you kidding? You are my hero." I leaned over to kiss her forehead.

"I'm going to let you rest," I said. "I'll be back tomorrow. Love you."

"Lov..." She was already asleep.

I closed the door quietly and went home to take a cleansing run.

I didn't need to go to the hospital the next day because Nessa was released. Nando picked her up and brought her to his house so her mother could tend to her. I stopped over there, just in time for dinner, bringing a large tub of purple mums that Nessa would be able to bring back to her own house when recovered.

Nessa had rested most of the day so she already looked better.

"You have pink in your cheeks, Nessa," I said. "That must have been so scary."

"Yeah, you know the one thing I'm afraid of," she said. "But for some reason, I only got shot in the arm."

"What was happening right before then? I followed you, you know, so I saw you get shot."

Nessa thought for a moment. "I remember trying to talk him down and then I remember hitting the pavement. Nothing really after that. I think the woman he was choking moved too fast and set him off."

"Good thing he wasn't aiming," I said.

Just then, Nessa's Abuelo came in, carrying our dinners on a tray. "Comer! Comer!" she said, smiling her toothless smile as always.

"I guess that means she wants us to eat," I said, blowing her a kiss and waving. "I wouldn't mind living here for a while," I said while I leaned over to smell my soup.

"This is *sopa de fideo* to Abuelo, chicken soup to you," Nessa said, slurping.

After dinner, Nessa and I watched *Twin Peaks*, her favorite TV show. It was a crime drama with eccentric characters and crazy dream sequences. I had never seen it before but it made sense that Nessa liked it. Nessa shushed me whenever I started to ask a question.

When the episode was over, I said, "I guess I'm going to have to watch this to see why you're so into it."

"Yeah," she said. "Isn't it great? David Lynch, the creator, is brilliant."

We talked for a while more and then I stood up to leave. I took her hand and said, "Before I go, I'm gonna get mushy and get this out of the way."

"Okayyy," Nessa said.

"When I thought I might lose you, I realized all the time I wasted not trusting you in our friendship. I know what a good person you are, and still I feared sharing my secrets with you. I'll try not to do that anymore."

I turned and left before she could answer.

Danny and I made the decision to see Keith at least once a week. I invited them both to breakfast the day after Nessa came home from the hospital.

"Good morning!" I welcomed them into the kitchen for breakfast of croissants, bacon, scrambled eggs, orange juice and lots of coffee.

"Good morning," they both said together and we shared a three-way hug.

Laughing, Keith said, "I am starving! Smells great."

"Dig in," I said, pinching Danny's arm. He turned to give me his dimpled smile.

As we ate, I told Keith about the shooting and the aftermath. I had already called Danny from the hospital. Of course, they both expressed relief for Nessa.

"Keith," I said. "I have a few questions for you, if you don't mind."

He nodded as he chewed his bacon.

"I saw you at the Phish concert," I said. You were standing next to my half-sister, Stephanie. How on earth did you meet her?"

Keith tilted his head and furrowed his eyebrows. "I don't know anyone named Stephanie. Your half-sister, you said?"

"That's another story. Apparently, my father and his secretary had a baby named Stephanie. I recently found out about her. But she was standing next to you at the concert. That really freaked me out!"

"I get that," Keith said. "But I just followed Nessa's car, bought a ticket for the concert, and stood where I could see you. That is wild that I stood next to someone you knew." He shook his head. "What are the odds of that?"

"That is crazy," I said. "I wracked my brain trying to figure that out."

I stood up and refreshed everyone's coffee. "There's another thing I am wondering about, Keith," I said.

"What's that?" he answered.

"How does your adoptive mother feel about you trying to find us?" I gestured toward Danny.

"I spoke with her the morning after we met at the Bronze Lady," Keith said. "She conveyed happiness for me but, of course, warned me to be careful not to get hurt. I never told her that I had stalked you. She would have been furious with me."

"I would love to meet her someday," I said. "Does she travel at all?"

"Uh, huh," Keith nodded.

"Would she want to come down to Sleepy Hollow for a visit sometime?" I asked. "What's her name?"

"Hetty Devlin," he said. "Short for Henrietta. And yes, I think she would love to meet you."

"Can we set that up, Keith?" I said. "Let's do it soon. Why don't you give me her address so I can send her a letter inviting her?"

"Sounds great."

"Danny," I said. "Maybe you and your parents could also come to dinner when Hetty comes?"

"You know my parents would love that," Danny said. "I'd better get going to help my dad. Keith, if you can, come by Clooney's some day for lunch."

"I will," Keith said, standing up and stretching. "It will be nice to see Mr. Clooney again. I'm looking for a job today. Maybe substitute teaching."

"Good luck, Keith," I said, hugging him. "See you tomorrow, Danny?"

"Sure thing," Danny said, waving to me at the door.

CHAPTER 23

FACING THE TRUTH

Danny and I still had two huge secrets left to reconcile—Timmy's death and Jake's suicide. We needed a private place to talk and decided to meet in Irvington to take Uncle Jimmy's boat out onto the Hudson. Danny steered the boat into the middle of the river and turned off the engine. The sun's bright rays did little to warm us against the cool autumn air. We both wore parkas but I put the blanket I brought over my knees. Despite the cold, I knew Danny enjoyed this as much as I did.

"Danny," I started. "Isn't a relief to have the baby secret out?"

"Yeah. I told my parents, you know."

"What?" I said in surprise.

"I had to tell them, Carrie," he said. "And wait 'til you hear what my mother said. She said she and your mother knew because your mother had hired a private investigator. Your mother knew something was going on. Even though we were so careful, they were all very suspicious."

"Well, that explains the picture I found in the house of a very pregnant me in Plattsburgh," I said.

"My parents were distraught to hear that you were raped," Danny said.

"Your father gave Nessa and me a plate of free apps the other night. Then he squeezed my shoulder and gave me that sweet smile."

"Him telling you he wants you to be OK," Danny said.

"So now that they all know that, what about our other secret? I have another thing to tell you."

"I just want this to end, Carrie."

I sighed deeply. "Me too. Which is why we have to talk about Timmy and Jake."

"Damn," yelled Danny to no one in the middle of the river. "I do *not* want to go there!" he said.

"Danny, we need to come up with how to tell our story. Chester saw us that night at the Lady."

"What? No one else was there," he was still yelling.

"Danny," I said. "I'm right here. Please don't yell."

"Sorry."

"Chester told me he caught a glimpse of us running away because he was in the cemetery. He heard people yelling but, I think, he thought he heard Timmy and Jake yelling. Before he got to the Bronze Lady, he caught a glimpse of us running away. When he got to the crypt, Jake was there kneeling over Timmy. That's what he told the police. Chester said he never told the police about seeing us because he cared for me. But I kept denying that we were there and he stopped talking to me for a while."

"Holy shit," said Danny.

"I don't know if we can count on Chester not telling someone else. I think we need to take control of the secret." I paused.

"And how do we do that?" asked Danny.

"Tell you the truth, I'm most afraid when Nessa finds out."

"Holy shit."

"Danny," I said. "You're going to have to expand your vocabulary."

We both laughed.

"Here goes," I said. "I think we need to sit down with Chester and Nessa and tell them the truth. That we arranged to meet Jake and Timmy at the Lady but only Timmy showed up. You confronted Timmy and he knocked you down. Then, he was kicking you and I pulled his legs out 'cause you couldn't get up in time. He fell and hit his head on the crypt. An accident and we should have told someone. But we were kids and ran like cowards."

Danny leaned his elbows on his knees and bent into his clasped hands. "That sounds OK. But what about Jake? We let my best friend take the fall for Timmy's death."

"That's a tough one, for sure." I looked up into the sky and felt the sun on my face. "We have to admit we were afraid and never thought Jake would be convicted. Then, we couldn't say anything because I was pregnant and—"

"I'm a piece of shit for letting Jake take the fall." Danny punched his leg.

"We have to be okay with whatever happens after we take responsibility," I said. "I can't believe that Nessa would let this pass even though I'm her best friend." I frowned. "I hope she stays my best friend," I said.

"Honestly?" Danny said. "I think Nessa will be impressed that you took responsibility. I really do."

"I hope so," I said, bundling up. "Let's head in. I am really cold."

"All right," Danny said. "Call me when you have the details of our meeting."

We listened to the rumbling of the boat motor as we approached the dock. I gave Danny a hug before I drove home to make some phone calls.

I sat outside Nora's office waiting for my appointment. I arrived early, anxious to talk about Nessa's shooting.

I have much to tell Nora. Where do I even start?

Nora's door opened precisely at 11:00 to signal the beginning of my session. By the time I walked in, Nora had already settled into her chair, her smiling face welcoming me.

"How has your week been, Carrie?" she asked.

"A crazy week—a secret revealed and a horrifying event. Nessa was shot in the arm during a domestic dispute."

She raised her eyes to meet mine. "Is she alright?" Nora said.

"Yes."

"How frightening."

"No kidding," I said. "I'd never seen anything like that. The bullet went in and out her upper arm. She was very lucky it didn't hit an artery. She didn't even need surgery."

"Wonderful news, Carrie," said Nora. "How do you feel about seeing the whole incident?"

I looked at one of the pictures on the wall. "I realized that I've wasted a lot of time keeping secrets. Basically, I hope she knows I'll be a better friend from now on."

"How will you do that?" Nora asked.

"Danny and I have two more secrets to share with her. There may be repercussions but the air needs to be cleared. I will share with you but I think Nessa deserves to hear it first." I paused, taking a deep breath. "Can we talk about something else, please?"

"Of course," she said. "Last week, you mentioned that you thought your mother knew about your pregnancy. Would you want to talk about that?"

"Did I tell you about the picture I found?" I asked.

Nora shook her head.

"My mother hired a private investigator to take the picture for her." *She saw through all my tricks: the pillow, the mono, and being too sick to travel home.*

"I discovered one of those old cigar boxes that I thought I had thrown away," I said. "It had a lot of silly little treasures. My mother kept it and I found it while cleaning out a closet."

"How do you feel about her knowing you were pregnant?" Nora said.

"You know, it's interesting. Over the years, Mother said to me that she always wished I had gotten married and had a baby. But she never said anything."

"But neither did you, Carrie."

"You're right," I said. "She probably waited for me to tell her. I wonder how different our lives would have been if I had told her."

Nora let me sit and ponder that for a few minutes.

I continued. "Danny just told me yesterday that he told his parents about Keith. And the rape. His mother said she knew about the pregnancy because my mother shared the picture with her. Everyone had secrets. Crazy," I said, shaking my head.

Nora said, "Were you surprised that your mother kept that picture for you?"

"I actually am. Relationships are so complicated. I might have missed out on a lot with my parents. I guess I made it tough for them to be close to me."

"Maybe they made it tough for you to be close to them, Carrie," Nora said. "It often goes both ways."

I nodded my head, thinking that Nora helped me realize so many things.

"Thanks, Nora. Can I get in next week?"

"Sure. Let me check my calendar." She walked to her desk. "Yes, I can do 10 next week, instead of 11. Will that work?"

"Great. See you then," I said, opening the door.

"Good luck, Carrie," said Nora.

I had almost forgotten what I still had to do.

CHAPTER 24

SECRETS EXPOSED

We had to wait another ten days for Nessa to heal from her wounds. When she felt healthy enough, I asked her to have dinner with Danny and me, but then requested that she call and invite Chester to come also. I suggested she ask Chester to give her a ride. I knew Chester would agree to that. He sent flowers and candy during her recovery and called her every day.

During my extra-long run that morning, I realized I had come to peace with what might happen to Danny and me. Even if we went to jail, I just wanted it to be over. Danny and I had carried those secrets for more than twenty years. It was time for the truth to come out.

Everyone arrived at 6 pm and I decided to serve dinner right away. I set up lasagna and salad, buffet style, with yummy Italian bread from Alter's Bakery and red wine, of course. Everyone loaded up their plates and sat down.

"A toast to Nessa," Danny said. "May you be 100% real soon!"

We all clinked glasses and took a sip, mine a large one to summon courage.

"Danny and I called you here tonight for a reason," I said. Danny, who was sitting next to me, took my hand.

"Are you guys getting married or something?" asked Chester.

"No, no, no," we said at the same time, then looked at each other and managed to laugh.

"Nessa," I said. "This is going to be difficult. Please hear this out to the end, OK?"

Her eyes shifted left, then right. "OK, Mija. What's going on?"

"It involves things that go way back to high school. Things Danny and I have kept from you."

"So why are you telling us now?" Nessa said.

"You deserve to know the truth."

"Okay, now you're starting to worry me."

"I know, I know," I said and took a deep breath.

"I'll start with you," as I turned to Chester. "I doubt that you have heard the news that I have discovered my stalker. Turns out, he is my son. His name is Keith."

Chester's eyes grew round and his mouth dropped open. "What?"

"I know you're shocked, Chester," I said. "But we never told anyone. Keith found us and felt confused and hurt because he thought we had just given him away because we didn't care about him. We explained to him what happened."

"What did happen?" said Chester.

"That we couldn't take care of a child," Danny said.

I turned to Chester. "But there's more," I said.

"More?" Chester said, incredulous.

"Yes. Keith isn't Danny's child."

Chester's mouth gaped. "I don't under—"

I cut him off. "Timmy raped me on Prom night when I left the party by myself," I admitted.

Chester reached for my hand. "Carrie, I'm so sorry."

"Thank you, Chester," I said. "I never told anyone except Danny about that either."

Danny cleared his throat. "So, we told Timmy and Jake to meet us at the Lady that night."

Chester glared at me, his nostrils flaring. "Then I did see you!" he yelled. "You lied to me, Carrie!"

He stood up to leave. "And did you lie to me about the journal, too?

"What journal?" Danny said.

"Wait, Chester," said Nessa. "I want to hear the rest."

"We were at the Bronze Lady before Jake arrived. Danny confronted Timmy about the rape and Timmy jumped him. When Danny was down, Timmy started to kick him and I pulled Timmy's legs out from under him. He fell and hit his head on the crypt. We ran. So, so stupid of us but, yes, we ran." I started to cry and looked at Nessa. "It really was a total accident. We never intended for Timmy to die."

Nessa stood up. She still had her arm in a sling and looked as wounded as when she got shot.

"Carrie," she said. "Oh, Carrie. Danny. How could you let Jake go to jail for something he didn't do?"

"I don't know, Nessa. Can you ever forgive me?" I pleaded.

Nessa stared at me with her serious cop-face. "I need to leave, Chester," Nessa said. "Let's go."

They stalked out, slamming the door.

Danny and I just held each other and cried. He stayed for another hour before he left.

Did I do the right thing? Should we have told them? What will happen to us now?

I didn't get any sleep that night. I couldn't get Nessa's face out of my mind when she heard the news about Jake being innocent. So disappointed in me. So angry.

To keep busy, I cleaned another closet and took a walk to the cemetery to visit my parents' graves. About an hour later, my phone rang.

"Hello," I said.

"Hi Carrie, it's Chester."

"Chester, I didn't think I'd hear from you so soon. Everything OK?"

"I saw you leaving the cemetery today," he said. "Did you visit your parents?"

"Yes," I said. After an uncomfortable pause, I asked, "Would you be willing to meet with me today? I'd like to talk. Anywhere you want. Anytime."

"Will it be worth my time, Carrie?"

Shocked by his abruptness, I sputtered, "Yeesss."

"All right. Let's meet at noon at the restaurant, Pickwick Post."

I agreed and hung up the phone. I immediately walked upstairs to my bedroom and took out the journal from the drawer in my bedstand. I hugged the journal to my chest.

Was I going to do this? I really didn't need to read his journal anymore. I already told him we were there. What should I say about disrespecting his privacy?

An hour later I sat in a booth at the Pickwick Post waiting for Chester. Both the middle fingers on my hands were picking at the skin on my thumbs. The journal lay on the seat next to me in a small paper bag.

I'm doing the right thing. Chester already knows anyway.

Chester walked drudgingly toward me, as if seeing me seemed totally unpleasant. He plopped down across from me, just as the waitress came to take our orders.

"Hi," I said to him. "What are you getting?"

Chester smiled at the waitress. "I'll have a Rueben on rye with an extra pickle and coke, please."

"I'll have the same," I said.

I waited for Chester to start the conversation but realized that was not going to happen. He knew this was uncomfortable for me and, I guess, he didn't care.

I placed the bag in front of him. "Open this," I said, "but wait to hear my explanation. Please."

Chester took the journal from the bag and brought it to his heart. He looked at me with squinted eyes and rubbed his hand over the book with longing. His reaction almost brought me to tears.

"Liar," he mouthed. "Liar, liar, liar."

"I know, Chester," I whispered. "I'm so ashamed of myself. Can I try to explain?"

He nodded twice, paging through the journal.

"That secret of ours honestly ate away at me. The guilt. Knowing Danny and I were involved in two people dying. It's what kept both of us away from here for so long. When you said that you saw us that night running from the Bronze Lady, it threw me into a tizzy."

"I knew I saw you," Chester said.

"Yes, you did. But I had to find out what you meant. I asked you about it but you wouldn't answer me. Then, I found the journal behind the rock. I was so afraid to admit I had it."

"Liar," he mouthed again.

"Chester, I have made some really poor decisions. Keeping your journal was a mistake."

"Not—" said Chester.

"You're right," I corrected myself. "Not a mistake. A really bad decision."

Just then, our orders were placed on the table.

"How much did you read?" he said, still looking through his journal and avoiding my eyes.

I hesitated.

"You owe me, Carrie."

"You're right," I said. "I stopped at the day after Timmy's death when you talked with the police. I felt like I had already invaded your privacy. I didn't need to know anything else. It must have been terrible talking to the police."

"More than terrible," Chester said, finally glancing at me. "Because it was hard to believe that Jake hurt his brother. I should have told them about you. My bad decision."

"I'm sorry if I put you in that position. Another thing I've felt guilty about." I said, reaching out to touch his arm.

Chester did not pull away but gazed at me with thoughtfulness in his eyes. "You know," he said. "We were so young and immature, weren't we?"

My hand moved to take his hand.

"I certainly was inexperienced," Chester said. "Not having any friends or knowing how to act. I was a mess in high school. And so, so lonely."

"Chester, I want you to know that you have always fascinated me." I smiled at his surprise. "You are so friggin' smart and interesting. I'm glad we're friends." When he didn't react, I said, "Or at least, I hope we're still friends."

"Carrie, I have wanted to be your friend since high school. We all made dumb decisions. The important thing is that people take responsibility for them. And you are doing that, my friend." He squeezed my hand.

I let out a huge sigh of relief that caused a few of the patrons to turn their heads our way. Chester and I chuckled and finished our meal, talking about mundane issues. It was a relief to not talk about something emotionally draining.

CHAPTER 25

JUSTICE FOR JAKE

The week went quickly and, sooner than expected, my appointment with Nora arrived. Nessa still wasn't talking to me or Danny and she stopped going to Clooney's. I called Nessa daily but she never answered. I dreaded sharing my secrets with Nora but figured the worst had to have been when we told Nessa and Chester.

I feel like I'm seeing Nora more than my friends lately. I hope that changes soon. I miss Nessa. I wonder if she misses me.

"Hi," I said to Nora as I sat down. "Well, I did it. I shared my biggest secrets with Nessa."

"How did she respond?"

"She reacted as I thought and we haven't talked in a week."

"How do you feel about revealing your secrets to her?" Nora said.

"Conflicted. In a way, I regret it because I shocked her but, at the same time, I feel OK because it's off my chest."

"Care to talk about it, Carrie?" Nora asked.

"Mmm," I muttered. "Would I have client/therapist privilege?"

"I am required to report something if you are a danger to someone else or to yourself," Nora said. "Is that the case, Carrie?"

"No. Neither. But I think I would prefer to wait until I hear back from Nessa."

"That's fine," Nora said. "How is Keith?"

"Keith is great," I said. "He came for breakfast the other day and I think I'm going to meet his mother, err, his adoptive mother sometime soon."

"That sounds lovely," she said. "Carrie, how do you think Keith might change your life?"

"I hope that he stays in the area," I said. "I guess that might be selfish of me and I hope his mother, Hetty, understands."

"Is it hard for you to call Hetty his mother?"

"Getting used to it. I'm trying to imagine the dynamics if I do meet her," I said.

"How do you envision your relationship with Keith?" Nora said.

"Keith speaks very lovingly of his mother. I've come to realize that I don't want to compete with her."

Nora nodded.

"I would like to be a close friend, maybe like an aunt." I nodded. "Yes, like an aunt. I've never been one of those either."

"That sounds like a good decision," Nora said.

"I also have been thinking about asking him to move in with me," I blurted.

Nora's head popped up from her notes. "Oh? Tell me more."

"I have that big house and he's my son," I said. "He's sick."

"There's a lot to consider with a decision like that," Nora said.

"I know," I said feeling a little deflated. "How would I decide?"

"It may be a great solution, eventually," said Nora. "Right now, you two are in a honeymoon phase, though. Maybe you need more time to learn about each other? Meet his mother?"

"Yeah, I guess," I said.

"Remember that taking care of someone with a terminal illness is very difficult, even with help. I'm not saying you couldn't do it. I think you need more time to figure it out."

"I feel like I've wasted so much time already. The idea of waiting may drive me to drink," I said, trying to make a joke and avoiding her eyes.

"Are you drinking, Carrie?"

"Sure, everyone drinks," I said.

"Not everyone drinks to escape from life's stresses. Do you?"

"I was," I admitted.

"Do you want to talk about it?"

"Maybe another time. I'm dealing with a lot right now."

"All right, Carrie. Our time is up for today."

"How about next week?" Nora said.

"Same day, same time?" I asked.

"See you then."

After a week, Nessa finally called me in the morning and very formally said, "Carrie, you need to meet me at the Sleepy Hollow Police Station today at 2 pm. Can you do that?"

"Yes, Nessa," my voice shaking. "I'll call Danny. Will you be there?"

"Yes." she said. "I suggest you contact an attorney." Then I heard a click signaling she hung up.

I immediately called Danny. "Danny! Nessa just called me and we have to meet her at the police station today at 2," I screamed into the phone.

"Ouch, Carrie," Danny said. "Bring your voice down about 10 decibels. What did you say?"

I repeated it to him. Complete silence on the line. Then—

"Shit," he said. "What did we get ourselves into?"

"Danny, I'm so freaking scared. I thought Nessa would talk to us before she went to her cop friends."

"I think," Danny said, "that I need to ask my dad to come with us. What do you think?"

"Have you told him everything about this part?" I asked.

"No. But I do not think we should talk to cops without someone at the police station who wants to help us," Danny said. "Carrie?"

"What?"

"Can you come to Clooney's right now? I will ask someone to keep an eye on the bar and we can talk to my dad in his office. He has to hear our side first."

"OK," I said. "I'll be over after I change. Give me about thirty minutes."

Before I opened the door of Clooney's, I took a look down toward the river, glistening in the sun. No one could possibly know what the day would hold. We would disappoint everyone we knew. How would I face Danny's parents again? It's a good thing my parents were gone.

I heard Danny's voice right away.

"Carrie," he said. "Want something to drink?"

"I do, but I'll have a Cherry Coke. Thanks."

"Let's go. My dad is waiting for us." Danny's shaking hand almost spilled my drink. I grabbed a few napkins and took the soda from him.

"Danny," I said, pulling him closer. "Please tell me we've done the right thing."

"Too late now," he said, pushing open the door of the office.

Mr. Clooney started out sitting back in his chair, smiling and almost relaxing. As we told him our story, he sat up straighter and, by the end, leaned forward on the desk resting his face in his hands. Even when I spoke, he never took his eyes off Danny. Danny stammered through the story, grabbing my hand at certain points, his eyes pleading with his dad to help us.

"Pa!" Danny yelled. "Please say something."

"I love you, Danny," he said. "You're my flesh and blood. But I struggle to understand how you let one secret lead to another and define your life that way. You two have really made a mess of things." He turned to address me.

"Carrie, do you have a lawyer? Your father's friend?"

I nodded. "Nessa suggested I contact a lawyer."

"You need to call him to go in with us," Mr. Clooney said. "I know he's not a criminal attorney but he can probably handle today's meeting. Or refer us to someone more knowledgeable."

I searched for Uncle Frank's number in the phone book and used the phone on Mr. Clooney's desk.

"Uncle Frank, it's Carrie. I need your help. I'm in trouble. Can you meet me at the police station today at 2?"

"Trouble? What kind of trouble, Carrie?" Uncle Frank said.

"Big trouble, Uncle Frank. Can you come?"

"I will have to move around a few appointments but, yes, I'll be there."

"Thank you," I said. I placed the phone onto the receiver and looked at Danny. He and his father had their heads together, Danny's father's arm around his neck, soothing Danny as he cried. Danny reached out for me as I began to cry again.

We certainly had made a mess of things.

Danny went home with his father to change into a tie and jacket and I stayed in the office at Clooney's. I did not want to run into anyone. I spent the time picking at my nails and watching a rerun of *Murder, She Wrote* on the small TV in the back room. Danny came back an hour later and found me a bandage for my bleeding finger.

At 2 pm, Danny, his father and I trooped into the police station. Uncle Frank was waiting for us. He introduced himself to Danny and Mr. Clooney. I told the officer at the front desk that we were there for an appointment with Detective Nessa Martinez. He told us to take a seat to wait.

The next five minutes were excruciating, waiting for Nessa. Every time a door opened, all our heads turned hoping to see her. Finally, I saw her very serious cop-face approach us. I felt shivers up my spine. I grabbed Danny's hand.

She herded us into an interrogation room. Uncle Frank had asked Nessa to let us talk for ten minutes. I explained to Uncle Frank and then—

I bent over before I got to the chair. *Oh my God, I can't breathe.* I started pointing to my chest and hyperventilating. Mr. Clooney led me to the chair, bent me over, and rubbed my back.

"Slow down, Carrie," I heard him say. "Let's slow your breathing down. Can someone get her some water? You're OK, Carrie. Calm down."

Danny knelt down in front of me so I could see his eyes. He whispered to me, "I'm here, Carrie. I'm with you."

After a few minutes, Nessa and another detective came into the room with some paper cups with water. I tried not to gulp mine and avoided her gaze.

"OK," said Nessa. "Let's get started. "We probably need to make some introductions. I am Detective Nessa Martinez and this," her thumb pointing at her partner, "is Detective Xavier Lewis." Lewis nodded to everyone as we introduced ourselves.

Nessa continued. "I have brought Detective Lewis up to speed on this case. What we want to know, right now, is why we shouldn't slap a whole lot of charges on you two. Fleeing the scene of a crime for one, and manslaughter for another."

My mouth hung open. I looked at Danny and his eyes were as wide as mine.

"We're here to exonerate Jake," I said. Nessa and her partner leaned forward to hear me. I must have whispered.

"We want to exonerate Jake and take responsibility," I said louder.

"Isn't that convenient," Nessa almost spat in my face, "since Jake isn't here to enjoy his exoneration, is he?"

"Ooh!" I said, backing up, almost tipping my chair.

"That's enough, Detective," said Uncle Frank.

"We're done here," Nessa said.

And, with that, she and her partner left the room.

After Nessa left us in the interrogation room, we sat there waiting for someone else to come in. Finally, Uncle Frank went into the hall to ask when we could leave. We were all surprised and confused that we were allowed to leave, without any charges filed.

I asked everyone if they could come to my house for more discussion but Mr. Clooney begged out, needing to return to the bar. Danny thought he should go home and talk with his mother. Uncle Frank had appointments. I went home alone.

As dinnertime approached, I realized I hadn't eaten since breakfast. I reheated leftovers and sat down to eat. The ringing of the phone startled me.

"Hi Carrie," Uncle Frank said. "I made a few calls and found someone whom I think will be able to help you much better than I can. He's a criminal attorney and a good friend. I trust him, Carrie. His name is Robert Tanner and his office is in downtown Irvington. Can I give him your number?"

"I guess so, Uncle Frank," I said. "I wish you could help though."

"I know, dear," he said. "But he knows his way around a courtroom much better than I do in these matters."

In these matters...

"All right," I said. "Thank you for coming with me today. It helped me to see you there."

"Let me know if you need anything," he said. "Take care."

As I hung up, I realized again that Danny and I were in way over our heads.

The next day, I received a call from Mr. Tanner. He asked me to come to his office that afternoon, without Danny. I agreed and he gave me the address.

Main Street in Irvington had changed in twenty years since I last visited. Another river town, it had gentrified a bit and Tanner and Tanner, Attorneys at Law, was located in an old bank building with its own parking lot.

Mr. Tanner was short, squat, and very round. Everywhere. I suppressed a smile. He looked to be around forty-five, bald, and the ring on his left hand told me he was married. He welcomed me into his office, offering coffee and then making it for me himself.

I found it comfortable to talk with Mr. Tanner. He laughed easily and I thought he might have passed as a Southern gentleman if it weren't for his prominent Brooklyn accent.

"So, Miss Peters, tell me about this trouble you're in," he said.

"Please call me Carrie. I think we have a real mess," I started to explain the whole story, starting with the rape and ending with Jake committing suicide.

"Hmm," Mr. Tanner said. "Carrie, I'm not going to sugarcoat this situation. You could be charged as an adult with involuntary manslaughter and fleeing the scene. Danny could be charged as an accomplice. I would ask for no jail time and probation. Heck, some judges are even sentencing people to community service."

"We just want to exonerate Jake and let this go," I pleaded. "What about Danny? I don't think he has a criminal lawyer. Can you help him too?"

"No, but I have a friend, George Walker, who might be able to take the case. Leave me Danny's info."

"Carrie," Mr. Tanner said. "Do you give me permission to proceed on your behalf? I will call this..." he checked his notes, "Detective Martinez to see if we can work something out."

"Yes, please. I should mention that she is my best friend. I haven't spoken privately with her since that night we confessed to her." I pulled on my hangnail. "It's a terrible spot I put her in."

"I will call in a few days," he said. "Stay close to your phone."

I thanked him and decided to stop at Clooney's on my way home. Luckily, I found Danny tending bar. I sat at the end of the bar so we could speak privately. The place was empty except for two other men at a booth.

"Danny, I just talked with a criminal attorney and I think you should too," I said. "I hope you'll get a call in a few days from a lawyer in Ossining, George Walker. Talk with your parents but I think we need to be ready. We don't know if we're going to be charged."

"OK, thanks," Danny said, as he wrote down the name on a napkin. "I'll tell my dad." He grabbed my hand. "God, this is so fucking scary."

"Call and let me know what your father decides," I told Danny. I left to go home.

Danny called the next day to let me know he and his father felt very appreciative for the name of the criminal attorney. George Walker's secretary had called and arranged for them to meet in his office that day. Such a relief that they were able to see someone so soon, but I felt distressed that Danny's family couldn't really afford the fees. All their money was tied up in the bar. I guess we all would worry about that later.

The next day, my attorney, Mr. Tanner called to say we were required to appear in front of a judge at the Village Justice Court in Tarrytown at 1 PM in two days. Mr. Tanner suggested that we meet in his office together with Danny, his father, and Mr. Wyatt the next day to talk strategy.

It was surreal for me, Danny, and his father to talk with two men about ways to keep us out of jail. Both the attorneys agreed that asking for exoneration for Jake was the right thing to do.

"Carrie and Danny," Mr. Tanner said. "Is it all right with you if we maybe bargain for different outcomes?"

"What do you mean?" asked Danny.

"The main idea is to keep you out of jail," Mr. Walker said. "True?

"True," we agreed, "absolutely."

Mr. Wyatt continued. "We do not know what they are planning. We need to be ready with different options."

"Like what?" said Mr. Clooney.

"The judge or prosecution," Mr. Tanner explained, "might suggest anything from jail time, financial restitution to a relative of Timmy's, or probation. I've heard some judges lately are assigning community service."

"I think I'd be fine with whatever punishment, except for jail," I said, seeing Danny nod in agreement. "I don't see how jail would be beneficial to anyone. It's not like we're career criminals."

"No," Mr. Walker said. "But the prosecution will contend you were involved in a wrongful death."

"So, can we bargain on your behalf?" asked Mr. Tanner.

"Yes." Both Danny and I answered at once.

"Wait," said Danny. "Will we talk again if the prosecution refuses to bargain?"

"Yes," said Mr. Tanner. "We will meet you at the courthouse at 12:45 PM. Make sure you look presentable and don't be late."

What do I wear to my death sentence?

That's exactly how I felt. What do I wear to show that I am sincere? That I will never hurt another human being?

I actually felt angry that Danny had it easy. He just needed a suit or a tie and a jacket. Should I wear a dress or would I look sexy? Should I wear a casual sweater and skirt or would that show I didn't take the proceeding seriously enough? Should I wear a pantsuit that wasn't really pretty?

I decided on a dress that reached my knees with a light sweater, stockings and low heels. Nothing too threatening. I found simple silver earrings in my mother's jewelry box and a matching bracelet.

Danny and his parents picked me up to drive to court. Danny and I rode in silence in the backseat. His parents didn't speak either. Only a three-mile drive, it felt like the longest ride I'd ever taken.

We arrived early at 12:30 PM, intimidated by the wide front steps and tall white granite columns at the entrance. We took seats on the benches outside the courtroom. A few minutes later, the two attorneys exited from offices down the hall, followed by a medium sized blond man and a woman, around my age, both carrying briefcases. As they walked toward us, I spotted Nessa and her partner behind them. Nessa didn't look at me, although I am sure she saw me. Everyone else looked at us sitting on the bench.

As I entered the courtroom, the similarity to ones I had seen on TV struck me. Lots of wood, huge side windows, and the judge's imposing desk at the front. We sat down on the left side of the courtroom and I turned to watch Nessa and her partner huddle behind the prosecution table on the right. The man and woman I had seen in the hall were evidently the prosecution team.

"Carrie, I'm freaked out," Danny said.

The bailiff cut off my response, "All rise. Court is in session. The Honorable Judge Zacharius Gibson presiding."

We remained standing until the judge sat down. Judge Gibson, a man of average stature, showed the appropriate amount of seriousness but had a kind resting face with dark brown eyes. I stared at his face and whispered to Danny, "Does he look nice to you?"

Danny just shrugged as we stood to face the judge.

"Mr. Clooney and Miss Peters," Judge Gibson began, "you are here to answer to the following charges: involuntary manslaughter, fleeing the scene of a crime, and obstruction of justice. How do you plead?"

Before we could answer, the prosecutor, Mr. Oates, stood and asked if he could approach the bench. Both of our attorneys and Mr. Oates hurried up to speak with the judge.

I watched them closely. I couldn't hear what they said, but I studied their body language: talking, nodding, talking and then more nodding. The three returned to their seats.

The judge spoke first. "Counselors, do you need to speak with your clients before they plead?"

"Yes, Your Honor," they answered.

We huddled at the defense table. Mr. Tanner said, "The prosecution has agreed to no jail time in return for guilty pleas. We think what he's proposing is very fair and think you should proceed."

Danny and I nodded and faced the judge.

"Mr. Clooney," Judge Gibson said, "you have been charged with fleeing the scene of a crime and obstruction of justice. How do you plead?"

"Guilty, Your Honor," Danny said.

"Miss Peters, you have been charged with involuntary manslaughter, obstruction of justice and fleeing the scene of a crime. How do you plead?"

"Guilty, Your Honor," I said quietly.

"Please approach the bench, Mr. Clooney and Miss Peters," the judge directed.

My knees were knocking as Danny and I walked about halfway from our table to the bench. We looked up at this man, who held our fate in his hands.

"Miss Peters, what do you want to happen today?"

"I want Jake's name exonerated," I said.

"Mr. Clooney, how about you?"

"I want Jake's name exonerated also."

"Why do you want his name exonerated?" asked the judge. "How do you know he wasn't responsible?"

I spoke up. "Because I was the one who pulled out Timmy legs after he attacked us."

"Miss Peters," he continued, "I understand you have a child from one of the victims that resulted from an assault?"

"It was not an assault, Your Honor. Timmy raped me. I gave up the baby for adoption. His name is Keith Devlin. He recently found me."

"Mr. Prosecutor," the judge said, "what are you sentencing guidelines?"

"If I may approach the bench, Your Honor?" The prosecutor walked to the bench and handed him a sheet of paper.

"Mr. Clooney and Miss Peters," the judge said, "have you willingly entered into a plea agreement?"

We glanced at our lawyers who nodded. "Yes, Your Honor," we said in unison.

The judge looked down at his papers and then addressed us. "This poor decision that you made as teenagers has had great repercussions on this community. A family lost both sons and had their name tarnished. I believe the sentencing guidelines agreed upon are sufficient to carry everyone's lives forward, never forgetting the losses of Timmy and Jake Benson.

"The first part of my sentence is that you make financial restitution of $50,000.00 each to Mr. Devlin."

Danny gasped.

"Next, since you remain a part of this great town, I sentence you to 120 hours of community service. Each. To be completed within a year. And last…"

Danny grabbed my hand. We were waiting for him to send us to jail.

"You both will be on probation for five years. That involves reporting to an officer of the court and maintaining a clean record."

I tried not to but I burst into tears. I heard Danny saying, "Thank you, thank you. We are so sorry," as he helped me back to our seats.

I watched as our attorneys went over to shake the prosecutors' hands. Mr. and Mrs. Clooney leaned over the railing to hug Danny. I sat there alone in my seat, wishing that someone cared for me like that.

I felt someone standing next to me and looked up.

"Mija," Nessa said. "You were brave. Thank you for taking responsibility."

"Nessa!" I exclaimed. "How I've missed you."

We embraced tightly and left the courtroom arm in arm.

CHAPTER 26

BITTERSWEET CELEBRATIONS

We certainly had a lot to celebrate but it didn't feel joyful. Danny and I had just admitted to a terrible crime and we were fortunate that we had not been sent to prison. We decided to go to Clooney's to decompress and be together.

I overheard Danny talking with his parents at the bar. "I hate to think you have to take out a second mortgage on the bar. I promise you I will pay that money back, Pa. You can garnish my wages."

"Talk about it tomorrow, son," Mr. Clooney said, patting Danny on the back. "Let's enjoy the moment."

Danny came over to sit with me, Nessa, and Chester. Nessa had called Chester on her way to the bar.

"I'm overwhelmed," Danny said. "How do you feel Carrie?"

"The same," I said. "Confused too. Our attorneys and the prosecutors must have figured that all out beforehand. Nessa?" I turned to look at her sitting next to me. "Did you hear them working out the deal?"

"Yes," she said. "I vouched for you two but only if you admitted your guilt. I would not be sitting here if you hadn't."

I turned to kiss her on the cheek. "And we will be eternally grateful, right, Danny?"

Danny nodded.

"How will they exonerate Jake's name?" I asked.

Nessa couldn't wait to explain. "Jake will be exonerated by something called 'No Crime', meaning that the crime Jake was convicted of was actually an accident, so no crime was committed. It's pretty slick," Nessa said.

"Who will exonerate him?" Chester asked.

"The Governor will have to do that," Nessa said. "It will probably take at least a year. I think your attorneys agreed to gather the paperwork and send it to him."

"We should celebrate when it happens," I said. "What if we dedicate a bench to his memory or something like that?"

"Yeah," said Danny. "Great idea. We could put one in the park or at the high school."

"Or both!" Chester added, very pleased when we all laughed.

"What about all those community service hours?" Nessa said.

"I know that Carrie already volunteers in town but I'm kind of excited about it," Danny said. "You guys have any ideas for me?"

We all started to brainstorm ideas, speaking over each other: "Volunteer fireman, library, working with kids at schools, teaching something at the YMCA across the street."

"Whoa!" said Danny. "My brain can only handle a few ideas at once."

"Hey," Chester said. "Now that all this is over, I'm wondering if you would come to my house on Saturday afternoon for a barbecue. My dad said it was time he met my friends." He was beaming.

"Chester!" we all said at once. "I think we all would love to come," Nessa said. "What time and what can we bring?"

"How about 3 o'clock," Chester said, "and you don't need to bring anything."

"What?" said Nessa. "Abuela would love to make Dulce de Coco for me to share. Think of Rice Krispies with coconut. Yum!"

"And I make a great potato salad," I offered.

"And I'll bring lots of beer," said Danny.

"OK," said Chester, laughing. "I give up." He stood up to leave. "I'd better get home and tell Dad we're having a party."

"See you Saturday, Chester!" we all yelled, waving.

"That is awesome," Danny said. "I'm happy for him."

"Actually, I'm happy for all of us that he's our friend," I said. Nessa raised her beer to toast. "To Chester!"

Chester welcomed our little group at the front door and ushered us out to the large glassed-in porch that ran the entire width of the house. His home, painted in warm tones of blue and green with lots of dark wood, gave off a cozy feeling. On the back porch lived a large ficus tree in the corner and big comfortable-looking chairs, begging to be sat in.

"Oh, please," I said to no one in particular as I plopped into the nearest leather chair. "Please, bring me something to drink. I'm so parched."

Everyone stopped where they stood and then burst out laughing.

"Chester," his father, Bram VanWert, said, walking in from the other room. "I did not know your friends would be so demanding! What would you like, young lady?"

I jumped up and could feel my cheeks turning pink with embarrassment.

"I, uh, uh…" I stammered. "Just a beer? Sorry, Mr. VanWert."

"Coming up," he said, as he introduced himself to each of us, shaking hands. "And, please call me Bram."

So interesting. He seems so confident, so different than Chester.

"Hey," said Chester, "who wants to play foosball? We have a table set up in an extra bedroom."

"No way," Danny yelled. "You're on!"

"Better be careful, Danny," Bram warned. "Chester's pretty good."

"We'll see about that," Danny said.

While Chester and Danny ventured off, Nessa and I talked with Bram about their family history in the villages.

"Bram," I asked. "How long have your ancestors lived in the area?"

"Since the 1700s. I know you are familiar with the Bronze Lady," he said. "But did you know that buried in that crypt is our great-great-great, plus about three more greats, cousin by marriage?"

"No," said Nessa. "That's something Chester never shared with us. He is so knowledgeable and interesting to listen to."

"He has always loved history, that's for sure," said Bram. "Never could get enough. I almost think that's what made his time in school so lonely. He loved his books too much. And the cemetery."

Nessa spoke next. "I've always told him that he is more than qualified to run for the Sleepy Hollow Historian position."

"He's mentioned that to me," Bram said. "But he's honestly afraid he would lose in an election."

Nessa and I looked at each other and frowned.

"Not if we ran his campaign!" I said and leaned over to high-five Nessa.

We all laughed.

"I'll leave it to you ladies then," Bram said. "I can bet he would be easily swayed by the two of you!"

Just then, Chester and Danny returned, Danny hanging his head.

Chester, pumping his arm, said, "Have you heard the saying by Winston Churchill, 'History belongs to the victors?' Maybe next time, Danny-boy," Chester joked, lightly slapping him on the back.

"Yeah, yeah," said Danny. "I need another beer."

"My treat!" Chester said. "Anyone else need a refill?"

"Sure," said his father and Nessa.

After the chicken was barbecued and Abuela's dessert devoured, we said good night to Bram. Chester walked us out to our car.

"I can't thank you enough for coming," Chester said.

"We can't thank you enough for inviting us," I said as the four of us shared a group hug.

As we got into the car, Nessa said, "Just so you know, Chester. Carrie and I are your campaign managers in the next election for Town Historian."

Nessa closed her door and we guffawed at Chester's reaction. His mouth dropped open and he waved his pointer finger at us as Danny drove away.

Did we just leave his first party ever? Good for you, Chester.

Nora sat patiently at my next appointment, waiting for me to start. When that didn't happen, she tried again.

"Carrie?" she said. "Are you ready?"

"Yes," I nodded emphatically. "I will tell you that Danny and I are not going to jail and we were given very fair sentences."

"OK, Carrie. I'm not supposed to act shocked but where is this coming from?"

I explained how I had pulled out Timmy's legs in a fight and he accidentally hit his head and died. I told her how we ran and remained silent as Jake was convicted of his death. We went to college, had the baby, and then Jake committed suicide. Still we remained quiet until Keith came and changed my life.

I continued. "Our sentence involves probation, community service and financial restitution to Keith, as Timmy's surviving child. I am really pleased about the financial restitution from me because it will help him with the cost of fighting the Huntington's."

"I'm happy for you that it's all resolved and behind you," Nora said. "What is the overall feeling you have now about that whole event of Timmy's death and all that came after it?"

"I carried so much guilt for so many years," I said. "We created such a fucking…"

My hand covered my mouth, "Oh my God, I am so sorry!"

Nora smiled. "It's not the first time I've heard a cuss word in session. Go on."

"The secrets we carried created such a mess of our and others' lives, I meant to say. Those feelings of guilt are why we eventually confessed."

I turned my head to look at the painting of the beach on the wall. "I am relieved, I am proud of us, and I am thankful for people who forgave us," I said.

"I would like you to realize that you have been resilient though all these years," Nora told me.

"Why?"

"Because you continued with your life in a successful way," Nora said. "You finished your education, taught school, reestablished yourself in your community, and have good friends surrounding and advising you. That shows me you are resilient."

"But," I said. "What about the anxiety? The debilitating feelings of guilt? The secrets?"

"All humans exaggerate stressors very easily in our minds. Your situation, extreme as it may have been, almost became a self-fulfilling prophecy through the anxiety and guilt. Those were your body's attempts to deal with what you felt was immoral behavior."

Nora paused. "But here you are on the other side! Just great. Anything else you'd like to share?"

I told her about our plans for community service and trying not to even get a speeding ticket while on probation. I also asked her about continuing to see her in therapy.

"Absolutely," Nora said. "My door will always be open to you."

As I stood to leave, I leaned in for a hug. Nora whispered in my ear, "Doesn't it feel good to share?"

She stepped back and smiled.

"I'll be back," I said, waving and closing the door.

CHAPTER 27

ANGEL INVESTOR

Six months later, the May sky was crystal blue and the flowers were budding on the tulip trees in Patriot's Park. Danny, Nessa, Chester and I gathered by the stream dividing Tarrytown and Sleepy Hollow. Danny and his father had brought the bench that Danny built as part of his community service hours. I had paid for the plaque that read, "In memory of Jake and Timmy Benson. Gone too soon." Nessa and Chester brought four tubs of purple and white pansies to set near the bench. Nessa walked over and nudged me. "Look who's here."

Turning, I saw my son, Keith, walking toward me with a big grin. My friends all greeted him with handshakes.

Keith said, "Thank you for doing this. I know the circumstances weren't something to celebrate but Timmy will always be my father."

"I think you are someone to celebrate," I said, giving him a hug.

<hr />

Danny and I kept a checklist after our arraignment of what we needed to do to make things right. Even after attending to all the details of donating the bench in the park, we were more excited than ever to set up the next event, a charity bike ride for Juvenile Huntington's Disease the following year.

In the meantime, I continued my community service by building up a library at Phelps Memorial Hospital in the children's wing. Danny and Chester built the shelves, I painted them white, and I chose the books for the kids. I started a Story Hour once a week for the children.

Danny decided to spend his time improving the houses of our senior citizens in both towns. He was paid with homemade lemonade and lots of chocolate chip cookies.

I was able to pay the financial restitution to the court who transferred it to Keith. How ironic that I ended up paying my son for the death of his father.

Danny, however, could not afford to pay the money and he resisted my efforts to talk about it with him until two weeks after the ceremony. We were eating breakfast at my house.

"Danny, have you figured out how to pay the restitution?"

"No." He sighed and glanced out the window. "I think Pa is going to get a loan."

He met my eyes and said, "I hate that, Carrie."

"I'll bet you do," I said. "Can I share an idea?"

"Sure."

I put my hands out, palms facing him. "Just let me get this all out. My parents left me a lot of money. A lot, Danny, that I will never use. I would, of course, leave it to Keith but there is a good chance that I may outlive him. I can't believe I am saying that."

Danny sat back in his chair, his hands resting on his stomach.

"Your parents are like family to me," I said. "Always have been. I would like to give them a gift of the money for them to use. Then, no loan."

Danny shook his head. "That is very generous, Carrie. But this is our problem. And, besides, I doubt the court would let someone else come in and just pay off my debt."

"But, Danny," I protested.

"Thanks, but no." The discussion was over.

But the discussion wasn't really over. The next day, I called and asked Mr. Clooney to come to my house, but not tell Danny. He sounded skeptical but agreed to come at 9 before he went to the bar.

I had coffee for him as he sat down at the kitchen table.

"Mr. Clooney," I said. "I'm sorry I asked you not to tell Danny but he doesn't want to hear my idea about paying the restitution. Did he tell you we talked about it?"

"No, he didn't. But this is our family issue, Carrie."

"I'm sorry, but you are my family. My parents left me a lot of money. I'm sure you don't want to discuss details with me, but I am sure you probably don't have this money lying around like I happen to."

Mr. Clooney hung his head. "What do you propose?" he said.

"I suggested I pay it outright but Danny thought the courts wouldn't allow that. This morning, I called Uncle Frank. He suggested that I ask if you would consider an investor in your company."

Mr. Clooney's head snapped up.

I knew I had his attention so I continued. "I would not want any shares or voting rights. Just an 'angel investor' as Uncle Frank said."

"And," I said, "any money I make from the investment would just go back into the business. And I could give you more than the restitution if you need to make any updates or renovations."

"Carrie," Mr. Clooney said as his eyes filled with tears. "You are one special lady. Let me go home and talk to the family. There's a lot to think about."

"You know," I teased. "I've always wanted to be part of the Clooney clan."

"You always have been," he said, hugging me before walking out the door.

Two days later, Danny invited me to his parents' house for dinner. They asked someone to man the bar for a few hours.

As soon as we sat down to eat, Danny's father brought out a bottle of champagne.

"We are celebrating tonight, Carrie!" he said. "We are celebrating that you are going to be a part of Clooney's Tavern on Main. We accept your offer."

"Wonderful. I'm so happy," I said. "I promise I'll be a very silent partner."

Danny leaned over to kiss me on the cheek. My plan had worked out.

CHAPTER 28

TAKING BACK MY POWER

Damaged goods. That's how Danny and I once described ourselves. Although Sleepy Hollow seemed large with many possibilities as a high school senior, it's true that every place seems much smaller when you revisit it as an adult. I realized over time that, although my body had aged, I reverted easily back to the broken teenager I had once been when I returned to Sleepy Hollow.

My run that sunny, warm afternoon brought me to the twists and turns on the roads in the cemetery. I passed my parents' grave and blew them a kiss, ran to the south to see the crumbling headstones of the Civil War soldiers and those by the Old Dutch Church. Washington Irving's grave came next and then down the hill, past the Headless Horseman bridge. Running along the Pocantico River, I turned to the west to travel up the hill and stopped at the Bronze Lady, the one who had such a deep influence on my life.

I walked into the little courtyard.

"Why did you have such a profound impact on so many lives?" I said out loud. "Why did we let such things happen to us and get out of control?"

I wish she could have said something, anything. But, of course, the statue didn't and the sudden realization that I had figured this out for myself shocked me at first.

Oh, I know why this happened.

"People have created these legends about you, that you're scary and cause horrific things to happen to ordinary people and their ordinary lives." I glared at the Lady. "But you're just a statue. We gave you all that power."

I approached the statue and lowered my voice.

"But I'm just like you. I have been a keeper of secrets. Always appearing to be solid, to be strong. I've let myself be eaten away by guilt. Well, you can keep your secrets. Mine are out."

I reached out to stroke the Bronze Lady's hand. "Fresh start."

ACKNOWLEDGMENTS

This story is a love letter to my hometown and to my parents who had the wisdom to raise me there until I left for college.

Readers who have lived in Tarrytown and Sleepy Hollow will notice many familiarities as well as some differences. For the purposes of the story, the setting is Sleepy Hollow, not North Tarrytown. They may recognize names of places, teachers, and friends with minor changes. Hopefully, all readers will feel the magic and energy of the towns with the diversity of cultures and abundance of history.

It seemed idyllic growing up on the banks of the Hudson River, which widens significantly at Tarrytown and Sleepy Hollow. The river remains a constant, always commanding respect. I remember looking out of my bedroom window to glimpse at the Tappan Zee Bridge and, even as a young girl, being filled with awe. I wanted this story to be as much about the towns as it is about the characters.

I also want to acknowledge those people who helped me along the way. Thanks to Ami Mariscal at MindStir Media for guiding me through the publication process. Thanks to my editor, Ericka McIntyre, my writing groups in Minnesota and North Carolina, and to my readers (Mindy Agnoff, Anna DeAngelis, Jody Hadlock, Gael Lynch, Jolan Marchese, JoAnn Moser, Tracey Smith, and John Stipa) for their advice and encouragement. Another shout-out to JoAnn Moser who traveled to Sleepy Hollow Cemetery to see the Bronze Lady and took an amazing picture there that graces the cover of this book! Thanks to my family and friends who understand my obsession with Sleepy Hollow!

My heart is full from the support of my family. My three children (Megan, Erin, and Michael) and their significant others (Jonathan, Jay, and Kate) have nudged me along to finish. My six grandchildren (Mia, Gemma, Penelope, Finn, Mila, and Willa) think I am really cool for writing a book! And thanks to Jack, who has always known that writing is important to me but now is my biggest cheerleader. I love you all!

CPSIA information can be obtained
at www.ICGtesting.com
Printed in the USA
BVHW040220190523
664429BV00004B/139